PUFF

SU

HURRICANE HORROR

The roaring of the storm had risen so that Jason could not make out separate noises, nor could he guess what any of it meant. The whole world was howling and banging round him. The ground vibrated. He clamped his hands over his ears, but that was not enough to shut it out. The noise seeped between his fingers.

The room was shivering, tugging at the ground like a gas ballon that wanted to be free. The floor tilted. Furniture shifted. The last upright chair rocked and tipped over. The big old sofa rolled a short distance until it got stuck in the rucked-up rug . . .

Yelling furiously, Jason tried to stand up, but the wind caught him and rolled him over. He hit something, made a grab for it, and was carried on. Pain lanced up one leg. He thrashed helplessly at the air as he felt himself being lifted and flung out into the boiling mass of the storm.

Some other books by Jack Dillon

SURVIVE! EARTHQUAKE ALERT
SURVIVE! FIRE STORM

SURVIVE!
HURRICANE
HORROR

Jack Dillon

PUFFIN BOOKS

For William

Special thanks to Cherith Baldry and Ian Locke

PUFFIN BOOKS

Published by the Penguin Group
Penguin Books Ltd, 27 Wrights Lane, London W8 5TZ, England
Penguin Putnam Inc., 375 Hudson Street, New York, New York 10014, USA
Penguin Books Australia Ltd, Ringwood, Victoria, Australia
Penguin Books Canada Ltd, 10 Alcorn Avenue, Toronto, Ontario, Canada M4V 3B2
Penguin Books (NZ) Ltd, Private Bag 102902, NSMC, Auckland, New Zealand

On the World Wide Web at: www.penguin.com

Penguin Books Ltd, Registered Offices: Harmondsworth, Middlesex, England

First published 1999
1 3 5 7 9 10 8 6 4 2

Text copyright © Working Partners Ltd, 1999
All rights reserved

Created by Working Partners Ltd, London W12 7QY

The moral right of the author has been asserted

Typeset in Bembo

Made and printed in England by Clays Ltd, St Ives plc

British Library Cataloguing in Publication Data
A CIP catalogue record for this book is available from the British Library

ISBN 0–140–38816–8

CHAPTER ONE

Jason Mitchell held his T-shirt away from his body and flapped it vigorously. The resulting breeze cooled him a little, but the effort of flapping wasn't worth it. He let go, and the T-shirt clung wetly to him. Sweat prickled in his hair and trickled down the back of his neck. Heat hung over the school yard like damp washing. No one felt like moving. The basketball players had given up shooting hoops. Even Debbie-Jean Allen hadn't the energy to parade past the boys and pretend that she wasn't looking. Somewhere in the distance, thunder muttered.

'It's coming, you know.'

Jason turned to see his cousin, Gordon, peering at him through misted glasses.

'What's coming?' Jason replied.

'A storm,' Gordon said. 'A really big storm, I'll bet.'

Jason shrugged. 'Can't be soon enough for me.'

The bell rang for the end of recess. All over the yard groups of kids moved, and broke up, and started straggling back towards the door.

'They had a storm at Cape Kennedy yesterday,' Gordon said excitedly. 'Did you see it on TV, Jase? And down along the Keys, a couple of days ago. Do you reckon we'll get one here, Jase?'

Jason stopped listening. They'd lived in Florida all their lives, and every year there were storms. Storms were a part of life. But try telling Gordon that. Jason had never known anyone worse than Gordon for getting excited about nothing.

Just ahead of them, kids were milling around the door into the school. Jason could hear Mrs Wyman's parrot-like screech above their chatter.

'Don't go back to your classrooms. Go straight to the assembly hall. The Principal wants to address all students.' And again, to a new group who had just come within range, 'Don't go back to your classrooms . . .'

Jason caught a glimpse of her, waving her

arms around. He felt hotter just looking at her. He wedged himself into the crowd and shuffled through the door and along the passage to the assembly hall, with Gordon twittering along at his elbow. Vaguely curious, he wondered what the Principal would have to say. Had somebody been complaining about student behaviour again, loud music and litter on the sidewalks, like always? Jason was ready to be bored, but it sure beat an hour of history, especially when he hadn't finished his assignment.

The Principal, Mr Johnson, was already waiting on the platform as Jason and the other students filed into the hall. He was a tall, thin man; winter and summer alike, he always wore the same grey suits and starched white shirts. And he never looked hot. Jason thought he must carry around his own personal, invisible ice-box.

Maybe it ran in the family. Mr Johnson's daughter, Lindy, was in Jason's class and was just as cool as her father. She was standing in front of Jason now, with not a single pale blonde hair out of place.

When the last of the students had slouched into the hall, the Principal tapped for silence on the edge of the lectern. The coughing, shuffling and whispering quickly died away.

'You may have heard on the radio or TV,'

the Principal began in his customary monotone voice, 'about the storms that have been breaking out all over the State over the last few days.'

Gordon jabbed Jason in the ribs, but not even he would dare to talk when the Principal was in full flow.

'Just a few moments ago,' Mr Johnson went on, 'I heard the hurricane watch signal over the radio. You all know what that means. It is quite likely that a severe storm will hit this area within twenty-four hours. Emergency plans are being put into operation, and those who can have been advised to leave.'

As soon as he mentioned the hurricane watch, a murmuring began to grow in the hall, and it swelled louder as the Principal went on speaking. At last he had to stop and rap the lectern. The murmur faded.

To his right, Jason sensed Gordon's stare boring into him. He deliberately ignored his cousin, denying Gordon the annoying opportunity to tell him that he'd been right about the hurricane. Jason kept his eyes fixed on Mr Johnson.

'Seeing that the situation is so serious, and that many of you may be leaving the area for the time being, it has been decided to close the school until further notice.'

Part of Jason felt like leaping into the air, waving his arms and yelling. Another part, however, felt uneasy. There had been bad storms before, sure, but the school had always stayed open. Maybe this was more serious than he had thought.

Jason shrugged. If it was, there was nothing he could do about it. And at least there wouldn't be any more history lessons for a while. With any luck, especially if there was storm damage, the school might stay closed until the end of term. Jason grinned to himself. What if the school was blown away? Wouldn't *that* be something?

Meanwhile, Mr Johnson's talk was drawing to a close with some boring stuff about sensible behaviour, listening to news broadcasts, and doing what your parents told you.

'. . . and any students who need to call home for their parents to collect them, may do so from the school office. The rest of you, take your belongings and go. Quietly! Dismiss.'

The hall began to empty. Jason knew he would need to call his Mom for a ride home. His family's citrus grove was more than ten kilometres out of town, and there was no way he was going to roast in any of the school buses they'd laid on. No way.

But when he turned to go to the office,

there was already a line of kids waiting, and it stretched all the way down the corridor.

'Come home with me, Jase,' Gordon said, tugging on his sleeve. 'You can call from there. Or Mom will give you a ride.'

Jason knew that getting into a car that had his Aunt Anora behind the wheel was probably more dangerous than the average hurricane. But he grunted his thanks, slung his bag over his shoulder, and left the school together with Gordon.

The heat outside was still stifling. The sky was an electric greenish grey, pressing down low over the rooftops. Thunder rumbled a long way off, and there was a distant flicker of lightning. A faint, hot breeze sprang up, raising tiny whirlwinds in the dust. A crumpled paper bag rolled past and Jason pounced on it to put it in a dustbin. 'You reckon you'll be leaving, then?' Jason asked his cousin.

'Sure. Mom hates storms. We'll go stay with Grandma for a while.'

Jason dropped the bag in the dustbin. 'I'd rather stay. A really big storm – it might be kind of fun.'

The two boys walked on, turning into the wide, tree-lined road where Gordon lived. Outside the house, a car was parked with its boot open. Gordon's father was arranging

6

suitcases inside. He stopped and mopped his forehead with a handkerchief, staring at a space that was too small for what had to go in it.

'Hi, Dad,' Gordon said. 'Guess what? They closed school!'

'Good. Go indoors, pack a few things, then help your Mom.'

Gordon shrugged at Jason and sprinted off up the path.

'Hi, Uncle Paul,' Jason said. 'Is it OK if I call home?'

'Sure. Go ahead.'

Jason followed Gordon up the path. In the porch he met Gordon's mother, all hot and bothered.

'Hi, Aunt Anora. OK if I call Mom? I need a ride home.'

'What? Oh – yes, yes.' She flapped a hand at him. 'I'd take you myself, Jason, but we have to pack the car.'

'I'll take him.' Gordon's sister Sally came out of the house carrying a pet basket in one hand. A tiny, hairy dog snuffled and complained inside. 'Here's Washington, Mom. And I've packed food and water. He'll be fine.'

Sally went to college. She had her driver's licence *and* a zippy red sports car for her last birthday. Jason had often wondered how a jerk

like Gordon managed to have a sister like Sally.
He grinned at her, and she smiled back.

'Make sure you come straight back here,
now,' Aunt Anora said, her brow furrowed.
'Your father won't want to hang around and
get snarled up in all the traffic.'

'Sure, Mom.'

Sally led the way to the garage where her car
was parked. There was a suitcase and a box of
books in the open boot. Sally slammed it shut
and got into the driver's seat. Jason fitted
himself in beside her. Maybe, if he worked
harder and got good grades, his dad would buy
him a car like this when he was old enough.

Sally steered the car out into the road and
through the estates on the edge of town. The
open-topped car made its own breeze, and
Jason started to feel cool for the first time that
day.

As they joined the freeway and began
driving north, Jason realized that the traffic was
much heavier than usual. There were long
queues at the petrol stations they passed.
Already people were starting to leave.

'So they closed the school?' Sally said,
tucking the little sports car in behind an
overloaded station wagon.

Jason told her what had happened that
morning.

'Will we see you at Grandma's?' Sally asked.

'Don't know. Nobody knew anything about a hurricane coming when I left home this morning.'

Sally made a snorting noise. 'Oh, come on, Jason! This has been building up for days. We don't all go around with our ears closed. I'd be surprised if your Mom hadn't made some plans.'

'Well, maybe. But I don't know what they are,' Jason said defensively. 'Anyway, Dad won't want to leave.'

'He's a fool if he doesn't.'

Jason grinned. Sally was one of the few people who could stand up to his dad. 'I guess he is . . . kind of stubborn.'

Sally smiled back at him. Jason's father was widely known as being harder to move than the Plymouth Rock.

Sally spun the wheel expertly, and the little car went bucketing up the dirt road that led from the freeway to the Mitchell citrus grove. On either side were rows of small trees, their fruit half-hidden in clusters of dark-green leaves. Drake Mitchell was expecting a record crop this year.

After a couple of kilometres, the trees gave way to an open space covered with grass, in the middle of which was a white frame house with morning glories twining on the trellis. A small girl bouncing a ball was making the veranda rattle. When she saw the car, she scrambled down the steps and ran towards it. 'Sally! Sally!' she cried.

'Bethy! How's my girl?'

Sally got out of the car and swept the child up in her arms.

'I lost a tooth,' Bethy said. She pulled down her lower lip and showed Sally the hole.

Jason groaned. There should be some kind of a law against cute little sisters.

'Clever girl,' Sally said, looking impressed. 'Will you put it under your pillow for the tooth fairy?'

Bethy nodded, and her eyes shone.

Sally put her down as the house door opened and Jason's mother came out.

'Hi, Aunt Abby,' Sally said. 'I brought Jason. They closed the school.'

Jason's mother brushed a strand of hair back from her forehead. 'It's serious, then?' she said, looking concerned. 'I've been listening to the news on the radio. Are you leaving?'

'Yes. Dad called Grandma. We're going there. What about you?'

'I guess so.' Abby Mitchell looked back uncertainly at the house and, as if at a signal, the door opened again and a man came out: Drake Mitchell, Jason's father.

'Sally brought Jason home,' Abby said, looking at her husband. 'School's closed. Paul and Anora are going to my mother's.'

'I hope you all have a good vacation,' Drake Mitchell said pleasantly.

'It's not a vacation!' Sally glared at him. 'Uncle Drake, there's a hurricane building up to hit this coast, or don't you know that?'

'Sure, I know.' Drake flicked a hand. 'We've had bad storms before. We always ride them out.'

'You mean you're not going?'

'Certainly not.'

'But Drake –' Abby began.

'Let Paul and Anora go if they want to,' Drake said. 'If they want to put up with your mother, who is a cantankerous old witch – and I don't care who hears me say so – and find their house looted when they get back, don't blame me.'

'Don't worry, we won't!' Sally said.

Jason hid a grin. One of the things he and his father always agreed on was their dislike of Grandma. He felt relieved to think he wasn't going *there*.

'There's plenty of work to be done here,' Drake said, 'especially as most of the workmen

11

didn't show up this morning. Jason, if school is out, you can help me. I've got a business here. I can't run off and leave it just because a few people are panicking.'

Sally had been angry, but now she was looking worried. 'You really mean it,' she said. 'You're staying?'

Drake clasped his hands behind his back and stood with feet apart, rooted, like one of his own trees. 'They always panic. We've had bad storms before and there was never any need to leave. I'm not leaving my property to looters. This is Mitchell land,' he said flatly. 'This is where we belong. We're staying.'

CHAPTER TWO

Thunder grumbled in the distance, as if responding to what Drake Mitchell had just said. Abby and Sally glanced anxiously at each other.

'Uncle Drake, please –' Sally begged.

'I meant what I said, Sally. We're staying. Or at least, I'm staying. If Abby wants to take the kids and go to her mother's, then go. I won't try to stop them.'

Jason was still sitting in Sally's car, but when his father said that, he got out hurriedly. The last thing he wanted was to go and stay with his grandma. To his relief, his mother wasn't going either.

'No,' she said, moving across to stand next to Jason's father. 'Do you think I could go and leave you here by yourself? When you don't even have enough sense to come in out of the rain?'

Drake Mitchell didn't bother to reply, and Abby sighed.

'Then I guess we're staying. At least . . .' She hesitated. 'Sally, would you take Jason and Bethy? I'll stay, but at least then I wouldn't have to worry about them.'

'Sure, Aunt Abby,' Sally replied, nodding.

Jason erupted. 'Oh, Mom! Grandma fusses all the time. She'll tell me to cut my hair and –'

'You argue too much, Jason Mitchell,' his mother snapped back. 'You'll do as you're told.'

Jason thrust his hands into his pockets and scuffed his feet. 'The food's really gross . . .' he muttered.

'Jason!'

'Let the boy stay,' Drake said. 'He's old enough to be some help around the place.'

'Sure, Dad, I'll help out,' Jason said, straightening up and trying to sound bright and eager. You could have enough of oranges sometimes, but they beat staying with Grandma any day.

'Just Bethy, then,' Abby said, turning towards the house. 'I'll pack her bag.'

'Are you sure about this, Jason?' Sally said.

'Yeah, I'm staying,' he replied.

'Uncle Drake . . .?'

Jason could see that Sally was going to start arguing with his father again. He could have told her it would do no good. But she never got a chance to say whatever she meant to say, because just then a man came round the side of the house. He was tall and lanky, with thinning hair and a hatchet face. Tom Hogan was Drake Mitchell's foreman. He gave Jason a brief nod.

'We've tied down what can be tied, Drake.' He paused, then added, 'We've been listening to the radio, out back. Reckon it's building up real bad. Robbins and O'Malley are leaving. Going to get their families out.'

His last few words were interrupted by the sound of a car's engine starting up. A jeep, with two men on board, drove round the side of the house. It slowed down as it passed Sally's car but didn't stop, and one of the men yelled something that Jason couldn't catch. The jeep disappeared among the trees.

Drake Mitchell shrugged. 'So that just leaves you and me, Tom. Do you want to go as well?'

'Nope.' Tom shifted the gum he was chewing from one side of his mouth to the other. 'Reckon I'll see it out.'

Drake gave a sly smile. 'Good man.'

Jason was still gazing down the road at the

spot where the jeep had vanished. He was starting to feel uneasy again. Bill Robbins was a young man, always joking and laughing; he'd married last year and there was a new baby in the house. Jason could understand that he wouldn't want to stick around. But Mike O'Malley was older, tougher; nothing ever bothered him. If he thought it was going to be that bad, then maybe they'd better start taking notice.

After a few minutes, the house door opened and Jason's mother appeared again. She was carrying a canvas bag in one hand and a teddy bear in the other. Sally took the bag and fitted it into the boot of her car alongside the box of books, and she sat the teddy up on the passenger seat.

Meanwhile Abby was looking around for Bethy. 'Now where has the child got to? Bethy! Bethy!'

Bethy staggered out on to the veranda. She was carrying Tiger, the Mitchells' enormous striped cat, clasping him round his middle. Dangling from her arms, Tiger looked like a well-dressed lady's fur wrap. Unlike a fur wrap, he was writhing and spitting and was in a foul temper.

'Want to take Tiger,' Bethy announced.

'Well, you can't,' her mother snapped.

'Grandma hates cats.'

'But Tiger's only little, he might get blown awa-a-ay!' Bethy wailed.

'We can take him,' Sally said. 'Do you have a cat basket? Grandma will just have to put up with him.'

Before Abby could reply, Tiger settled the argument by giving a massive wriggle, leaping out of Bethy's arms and over the veranda rail, and racing round the side of the house. Bethy started to run after him, but she fell over and broke into ear-splitting howls.

Jason took off after Tiger and reached the corner of the house just in time to see a tabby streak vanish among the orange trees. Jason pounded in pursuit but, by the time he reached the spot, there was no sign of Tiger.

'Here, kitty, kitty, kitty,' he called, without much hope. Even at the best of times, Tiger only came in response to the banging of the food bowl, and not even then if he had something better to do. Now Jason thought they would be lucky if he came back before dark.

He returned to the front of the house, where he found Sally trying to comfort Bethy and his mother looking on, exasperated.

'This is all your fault!' she was saying to his father. 'Stubborn as a whole herd of mules!'

Bethy was sobbing noisily.

Drake Mitchell strolled down from the veranda. 'Elizabeth, stop that noise at once.' He took a few coins out of his pocket. 'Now, you be a good girl and go visit Grandma with your Cousin Sally. Here's some money to buy candy. When this is over, your Mom and I and Jason will come and fetch you, and we'll all go to the beach. OK?'

Bethy stopped bawling and looked at her father. It's a good deal, Jason thought. Go for it. But Bethy's face was set mutinously. Clearly it was not OK.

'I want Tiger,' she said.

Suddenly Jason felt like laughing. He had just noticed something he had never seen before: when she was determined to have her own way, Bethy looked exactly like their father.

Jason squatted down beside her. 'Bethy, *I'll* look for Tiger,' he said. 'I'll take really good care of him, honest.'

Bethy weighed him up. 'Promise?'

'Promise.'

'Teddy's waiting for you,' Sally said hopefully. For a few seconds Bethy still hesitated and then, without saying any more, she marched over to Sally's car and got in, cuddling the teddy bear.

Abby let out a long sigh of relief and bent over to give Bethy a kiss, while Sally slid behind the wheel and fixed the seat-belt.

As Sally started the engine, Jason had a sudden impulse to say, 'Wait for me, I'm coming with you.' But his mum was making a fuss about messages for Aunt Anora and reminding Bethy to be sure to clean her teeth. His father was looking on with a neutral expression.

Jason watched and said nothing as the little red car swept round in a wide circle to face the road again. Bethy was waving madly, quite happy now, and he waved back. He stood beside his mother and father and watched the car, like the jeep before it, disappear into the tunnel of trees. For a moment he kept seeing one or two flickers of scarlet, but then they were gone.

A light wind rose and swept across the trees, turning the leaves back and revealing the half-grown fruit. A few fat drops of rain spattered on the open ground. Tom Hogan slapped his dusty cap across his legs, turned and set off towards the sheds behind the house.

'Well, that's that,' Drake Mitchell said, turning to go back into the house. 'Abby, why don't you fix lunch?'

CHAPTER THREE

For an hour the rain held off, but when the Mitchells and Tom Hogan sat down to eat in the kitchen the sky was so dark that they needed to put the light on. Through the open window they could hear the continuous rustling of the wind in the trees.

Abby had microwaved pizzas and tossed a salad. She was eating quickly, left-handed, while with the other hand she scribbled something on a piece of paper.

'What's that, Mom?' Jason asked, demolishing half of his first slice of pizza in one mouthful.

'Shopping list. If the storm's bad, the roads might be blocked and, if everybody leaves, the stores will be closed. I want enough extra food to get us by until things are back to normal. This thing could last a week.' Her voice dropped to a murmur. 'Bread . . . butter – better get two packs, no, three – canned meat . . .'

'Put down chocolate-frosted doughnuts,' Jason said.

His mother shot him a dirty look. 'We're talking survival here, Jason, not tooth decay.' She went on writing, then stopped to say, 'Drake, what about the storm shutters? Oughtn't they to be up over the windows by now?'

'They're stacked outside the garage,' Jason's father said. 'I'll see to it after lunch. And the roof straps. Jason, you can help.'

Jason grunted. He was stuck with it now, he supposed. He'd chosen this over going to Grandma's, so there was no point in complaining. He could feel his back aching already, trying to lift the heavy shutters into place.

Abby's list was getting longer. 'Tom,' she said, 'will you take the pickup truck and collect all this?'

'Sure, Mrs Mitchell,' Tom said, swallowing a mouthful of coffee.

'Can I come?' Jason said, scenting escape. 'I can help carry stuff.'

His mother was not listening to him; she

was concentrating on her list. At last she threw the pencil down, exasperated. 'Oh, I don't know, Tom. Just get what you can. Canned foods and packets mostly – whatever will keep. Nothing that needs to go in the ice-box. Things we can eat cold if we have to.'

Tom took the list and stuffed it into his shirt pocket. 'Sure, Mrs Mitchell. No problem.'

'There are bound to be power cuts,' Abby said to Drake. 'It's happened before. In a really bad wind, the power lines are the first to go.'

Drake Mitchell put down his fork and pushed his empty plate away. Nothing ever spoiled his appetite. 'Better get batteries, then, for the radio and the flashlights. And a gas canister for that old camping stove.' He took a roll of money out of one of the pockets of his baggy jeans and pushed it across the table towards Tom.

Tom got up from the table. Jason swallowed his last bite of pizza and followed him out. No one had exactly said he could go – but they hadn't said he couldn't either. He stopped on the veranda as he heard his mother calling him back.

'Yeah, Mom?' He took a step or two back into the house. It was going to be the storm shutters for sure.

'Jason – don't forget cat food for Tiger.'

Jason grinned. 'Sure thing, Mom.'

Tom Hogan was already driving the pickup truck round from the garage to the front of the house. Jason briefly looked up at the skies. Another flurry of light rain splashed into the dust, but the downpour was still holding off. Jason sprinted across and hauled himself up into the cab. Tom gunned the engine, and the truck lurched along the dirt road.

It was gloomy in the tunnel of trees. Tom snapped on the lights. On each side the trees were moving, swaying gently, their leaves rippling back and forth. Rain spattered across the windscreen in a single gust and then stopped again.

Jason started fiddling with the truck's radio to see if he could get a weather report. There was a lot of static, and he had found nothing better than crackly dance music when Tom turned the truck on to the freeway. Jason's hand dropped away from the radio controls.

'Wow!' he said. 'Will you look at that!'

On the opposite side of the freeway, going north, was a continuous stream of traffic, mostly cars, with a few trucks and camper vans. They were moving fast, bumper to bumper, and now and then there would be a clot of slower-moving traffic. In one place, where the cars had slowed, vehicles were piled up behind a station wagon that had slewed sideways across the road. Jason could hear horns blaring.

Twisting around in his seat, he could see that on the other side of the road temporary signs had been put up, showing drivers which way to go. Not that there was much need, Jason thought. Everyone knew. North. Out of here. *Away* from the storm.

There was no traffic at all going in the same direction as Tom and Jason and the truck. It was almost surreal. Somewhere inside him, Jason felt weird: to be moving south, against the flow. The passing cars continued relentlessly on. Did any of the drivers wonder about the idiots going the wrong way? If they did, they gave no sign of it, not signalling or stopping. Tom was concentrating on driving the truck, and his silence added to Jason's feeling of uneasiness.

The sky had grown darker still but, in place of the grey blanket that had covered everything earlier in the day, Jason thought he could see movement overhead, as if great masses of cloud were shoving against each other. Wind was bending the few trees by the side of the road. Rain started to fall again, a light drizzle that was just enough for Tom to switch on the windscreen wipers.

The store nearest the Mitchell home was just off the freeway, before you came to the town. There was a supermarket, a filling station, and a half dozen smaller stores, all sharing the same car park. Jason had been there hundreds of times before. But this time, as soon as Tom turned off the freeway, Jason could see that something was wrong. There were no other cars in the car park. The supermarket was closed, with metal grilles pulled down over its doors and windows.

Tom halted the truck in front of the supermarket and Jason got out, shivering in the cold rain. He hadn't bothered to put on anything warmer than the T-shirt he had been wearing at school.

Tom joined him and they rattled the grille over the supermarket doors. It held fast.

'Reckon they left, too,' Tom said.

'What are we going to do?' Jason scanned the other buildings.

'I'll take a look round the back,' Tom answered slowly.

Hands in his pockets, Tom loped towards the corner of the supermarket. Jason watched him go out of sight, then turned the other way. A candy store, a hairdresser's, a drug store – all locked and silent like the supermarket – and there was no sign of anyone around. Jason tried shouting: 'Hi! Anyone home!' – but there was no reply.

He went back to the truck. Tom reappeared a minute later, shaking his head. He got into the cab and started the engine.

'Let's go.'

Jason half expected him to turn for home, but instead he kept going towards the town. On the other side of the freeway the traffic was thinning out, and what was left moved faster, as if the drivers were scared of being left behind. The rain was getting heavier.

Just before the speed limit began, on the outskirts of the town, Tom turned on to a narrower road that led towards the beach. There was no traffic here either, and the houses they passed all looked empty, closed up.

Then Jason heard an engine snarling behind them, and a siren cut in, the wailing growing closer. Looking behind him, he saw a couple of state troopers, the lights of their patrol car flashing madly. 'Uh-oh,' he said.

Tom pulled over but kept his engine running. The cops pulled in behind; one of them got out and came to speak to Tom through the window of the pickup truck.

'You're going the wrong way, mister,' he said, taking off his reflective glasses.

Tom shifted his chewing gum over to the other side of his mouth. 'You seen any stores open, officer?' he asked.

The cop gave him a dirty look.

'Haven't you heard the warnings?' he said. 'A storm's going to hit this coast really soon now. A big storm. Everybody's leaving.'

'My boss ain't leaving,' Tom replied.

'Then your boss is out of his mind. And so are you. This your kid?'

'Nope. My boss's boy.'

'This is no place for kids,' the cop said. 'You turn around right now and get out of here.'

Tom hesitated for a moment as if he was considering whether to argue, but then he said calmly, 'Sure, officer.'

The cop stood back and watched as Tom manoeuvred the pickup truck round and set off along the road, back the way they had come. Jason could see the other man, still in the car, talking into his radio.

'Mom's going to kill us,' he said, thinking of what she would say if they went back empty-handed.

But a couple of minutes later, instead of rejoining the freeway, Tom turned the truck along another side-road that snaked round a dune with a couple of windblown sand pines. On the other side, a gentle slope led downhill to where, in the distance, Jason could see the beginning of the beach motels and cabins. Tom drove into another car park.

At first glance it was just like the other place where they had stopped. A filling station, a couple of tacky souvenir shops, and another small supermarket.

At second glance, though, it was different. The metal grille that had been pulled down over the supermarket windows was twisted and partly lifted. An enormous black star splashed across the window showed where the glass had been broken.

'Sheesh . . . what happened here?' Jason said.

Tom cut the engine, but he didn't move to get out of the cab. At last he spoke. 'Looters.'

CHAPTER
FOUR

Jason started to get out of the cab, but Tom grabbed his arm.

'You stay right here,' he said. 'Those guys could still be around. I'm going to take a look.'

He slid down; Jason watched him crossing the car park, looking warily around him, and then step carefully through the hole in the glass. He disappeared inside the supermarket.

Left alone, Jason wondered if the looters had been real thieves or just ordinary people like themselves, desperate for supplies and finding all the stores shut. They certainly hadn't wasted much time. Jason wondered where the state troopers had got to, and why they weren't here instead of bothering drivers who were just minding their own business.

29

Then he heard Tom calling. He had reappeared at the window and was beckoning to him. Jason jumped down from the cab and ran across the car park, the rain lashing down cold on his bare arms.

'You mind that glass now,' Tom said, as Jason picked his way through the hole. 'Reckon there's nobody here now. But I don't know if we can get what's on your mom's list. There's not that much left.'

Moving away from the broken glass, Jason took a good look around at the inside of the supermarket. There were no lights on, and it was so dark outside that it took a minute or two before he could make out anything in the gloom. When he did, he saw rubbish strewn along all the aisles and over the shelves – all of which were nearly empty.

'Hungry, weren't they?' Jason said to himself.

'Forget the list,' Tom said hurriedly. 'See what food you can find. I'll look for batteries and gas canisters.'

Jason looked around for a trolley, before he realized that pushing it through all the rubbish would be more trouble than it was worth. He took a carrier bag from one of the checkouts instead, and set off down the nearest aisle.

Everything was quiet, but Jason felt uneasy.

His own movements sounded too loud and they echoed with every step he took. He hoped Tom was right when he said the looters had gone. Jason didn't want to meet the people who had been so desperate that they had smashed that window.

He saw that the freezers and chilled cabinets were all switched off and empty, as if the store's owners had cleared them before they left. The dry goods on the shelves had gone, but there was enough mess left behind for Jason to see what had been there: flour, cereal and crunchy pasta shells lay underfoot.

He found three or four dented tins of frankfurters — his father hated frankfurters — and put them in his sack. A little further along, he came to tuna fish, and then a single tin of tomato soup that had been half hidden by a split packet of rice.

'Yuck,' he said aloud, but he took it anyway.

In the next aisle was a real find: a whole section full of pet food. The looters obviously didn't have any cats. He filled the rest of his sack with Tiger's favourite and took it back to the window. He could hear Tom moving about but couldn't see him, so he left the sack next to the hole, took another and set off again.

In the next aisle was a plastic bin that had held sweet biscuits, now empty of everything except some broken pieces at the bottom. Jason scrabbled them up and put them into a paper bag. Nearby there had been bread, but a few white and brown crumbs were all that remained; there was nothing left that was fit to eat. He found a few packets of dry biscuits and took those, some candy bars and a couple of packets of chewing gum. Tom would like those, and, Jason thought cunningly, his mum wouldn't mind him eating sweets if there was nothing else.

When he had filled the second sack and brought it back to the window, Tom was waiting with a gas canister in his hand.

'No batteries,' he said. 'I reckon we should get out of here.'

Jason wondered what they ought to do about paying for the food. There was no one here to take any money. If they just left, were they any better than the looters? Not knowing what else to do, he went to the nearest checkout and wrote on a paper bag: 'We took some food and stuff. We'll pay for it later. Jason Mitchell.'

Outside, against an ever-darkening sky, the rain was sweeping across the car park in waves, driven by the rising wind. The sand pines on the dune were bending in front of it.

'It's getting worse,' Jason cried out, against the noise.

'Sure is. Don't reckon that storm's far off, now.'

Tom picked up the other sack, ducked out through the broken window and sprinted across to the truck. Jason grabbed his own sack and followed, dodging the stinging drops as best he could. By the time he reached the shelter of the cab, gasping from the cold, he was soaked through. He was shivering as Tom started up the engine and moved off.

At the exit from the car park, Tom slowed down in case there was traffic on the road. The truck was facing the downward slope that led to the beach in the distance. Jason looked out through the windscreen. He could see the pale line of sand, contrasting with the dark clouds, and waves rolling in, higher and higher.

Jason had only one glimpse before Tom spun the wheel and pressed the accelerator. The truck swung out into the road, rainwater spraying up from its wheels. As they raced off in the opposite direction, Jason could no longer see the beach or the waves, but all the same he had a nasty feeling that they might come racing up behind him at any moment, foam washing round the truck's wheels, rising until it stopped the engine and swept them away to sea. He felt colder still at the thought of that freezing sea, and he made himself watch the road ahead, through the driving rain, instead of trying to look behind him.

It took ages before they reached the freeway again. The road was almost free of traffic now. The few cars that were about raced past at incredible speed, the road ahead free of obstructions. Wind was tugging at the advertising hoardings alongside it; here and there they were flapping as if about to be carried away at any minute.

'Wind's getting up,' Tom said quietly, and Jason strained to catch what it was he was saying.

About half way to the turnoff for the Mitchell house, they came to a car that was pulled in by the side of the road; its bonnet was up. As the pickup truck drew closer, the driver straightened up from where he had been poking around at the engine, and stepped into the road, waving his arms over his head. He was soaked through and water trickled down his face.

Tom frowned and looked as if he might sail straight on by, but then he slowed down and stopped, pulling up alongside the stranded vehicle.

'Car's broken down,' the driver shouted. 'Can you give us a ride out?'

'Sure,' Tom said. 'But I'm not going far.'

Jason thought the driver hadn't heard the last few words. He darted back through the rain to his own car and opened the door. A woman carrying a baby got out, and Jason squeezed over next to Tom, jamming himself against the hand-brake so that there would be room for her in the truck's cab. She handed the baby up to him and then climbed up herself. The baby batted Jason in the eye.

'Sorry,' the woman said. She was young, not much older than Sally, and pretty. 'He's getting restless.'

Jason handed the baby back, and the car driver – the woman's husband, Jason supposed – slung a couple of bags into the back of the truck and then climbed up after them. Tom set off again.

'That was really scary,' the woman said. 'We were late leaving, on account of looking for somewhere to fill up with gas, and then the car broke down and Bob couldn't fix it. That's Bob, my husband, in the back. I'm Ellen, and this is Zack.'

'Hi,' Jason said, smiling. 'Hi, Zack.'

Zack grabbed his hair and pulled until Jason's eyes watered.

'Don't mind him, he does that a lot,' Ellen said fondly.

She chatted on, describing their frantic bid

to get out of town, as the truck sped purposefully along the freeway. Jason got tired of being thumped by Zack, so he twisted around in his seat to get at the food behind it, and he gave Zack half a chocolate-chip cookie. Zack stuck it in his ear and gurgled cheerfully. At least he wasn't screaming, Jason thought.

When the truck started to slow down again, Jason didn't see why at first. They still hadn't reached the turnoff for the citrus grove. Then he saw a man jogging by the side of the road, facing them, heading for the town. He was wearing a tracksuit, and for a minute Jason had the crazy idea that he was just out for exercise.

Tom stopped the truck, but he kept the engine running. He leant out of the window and called out. 'Hey! Want a ride?'

The jogger pulled up, panting. Now that Jason got a good look at him, he could see he was too fat and out of breath to be enjoying this sort of thing for his health.

'You going into town?'

'Nope.' Tom gestured up the road. 'That way. Inland.'

The jogger shook his head. 'I've got to go back into town. I've got to find my wife.'

'Maybe she left already,' Ellen said kindly, craning towards the open window.

'Don't reckon so. I had the car, and then I

ran out of gas.' For a moment he leant one hand against the side of the truck, getting his breath back and wiping the rain off his face with the other hand.

Tom said, 'You'd best come with us.'

The jogger looked up at him. Jason could see in his face what nobody was saying: if his wife had stayed in the town, she might be dead before her husband could find her. It was the first time Jason had ever thought about somebody dying in the storm, but he suddenly pictured the wind striking the town, pictured windows shattering and roofs torn away, and the people left behind with nowhere to shelter. Would it really be as bad as that?

The jogger shook his head again. 'Thanks, but I've got to get down there.'

The man turned and jogged off along the road. As they moved away, Jason watched him until he disappeared into the driving rain, and he wondered if the man would reach the town in time. And what he would do if he did.

CHAPTER FIVE

Tom slowed the pickup truck and turned into the dirt road that led to the Mitchell house.

'Hey, where we going?' Ellen asked, suddenly disturbed from her mutterings by the change in direction.

'My boss's place,' Tom replied coolly.

Ellen seemed quite happy about that. She bounced Zack on her knee and started singing a nursery rhyme to him.

The tunnel made by the trees pitched the cab into blackness. Tom flicked on the truck's overhead light. The trees lashed from side to side. Already there were branches in the road, but the pickup lurched over them. Leaves whirled in the air and stuck to the windscreen.

The house looked shut up and deserted behind a curtain of rain. The roof straps were in place and storm shutters blanked out all the windows. Someone had cleared the garden furniture off the veranda, and Bethy's swing from its place near the corner of the house. There was no sign that anyone was there.

When Tom pulled up, Ellen's husband Bob jumped down from the back of the truck and ran round to the cab.

'Where've you brought us?' he shouted through the rain. 'You said you'd take us out!'

'I said I wasn't going far,' Tom replied impassively. 'This is my boss's place. You can –'

'We can't stay here!'

Ellen dumped Zack on Jason's lap and got down from the cab. 'Bob, don't!' she said. 'It was kind of these folks to bring us this far.'

Yeah, sure, Jason thought, wriggling across to the door and managing to get down with Zack, tucked under one arm, clinging painfully to his T-shirt. Thankfully, he handed the baby back to Ellen.

The front door swung open and Abby Mitchell stepped out, peering through the rain to see what was happening. 'What took you so long?' she called.

Jason dashed across to join her. 'The store was closed. But we found another, and that was

39

looted. And we saw really big waves, Mom, like they would cover the beach! And then –'

He broke off as Bob stopped arguing with Tom and ran across to the foot of the veranda steps, where he stood glaring up at Jason and Abby.

'We've got to get out of here!' he yelled. 'This storm's going to hit big time any minute!'

'Take it easy.' Drake Mitchell appeared behind Abby in the doorway. 'Come up on the veranda out of the rain, and we'll talk this over.'

Bob looked at the Mitchells' veranda as if it was going to turn into an alligator and bite him, but Ellen came up the steps, smiling from underneath a waterproof jacket she held, shielding her and the baby, and shook hands with Drake and Abby. Bob followed her, glowering. He was well built, a head taller than Drake, with shoulders like a football player, but Drake didn't look fazed at all.

'Well, we don't intend to leave,' Drake said, when Ellen had sketched out the story of their car breaking down in mid-flight and how Tom had picked them up in the truck. 'You folks are welcome to stay with us as long as you like.'

Oh no, Jason thought. Not with that kamikaze baby! To his relief, Bob seemed determined to get away, though for different reasons.

'It isn't safe here any more,' he shot back.

'You folks must be crazy to stay. We're getting out. Can we hire your truck?'

Jason could see his father was going to refuse. He could also see that Bob's fists were clenched, as if he might start using them at any minute. Then Tom, who had been unloading the supplies, set down the gas cylinder by the door, and said, 'Suppose I drive them out? I could drop them off somewhere safe and then, if I can, come back.'

Drake Mitchell thought about his suggestion for a minute and then nodded slowly. Bob relaxed and looked less angry. Ellen thanked everybody.

'But, Tom,' Abby pleaded with Drake's head foreman, 'if it's dangerous, don't try to get back. Don't take risks. We'll be fine.'

Tom gave her a long look. 'You're sure you won't come along, Mrs Mitchell? You and Jase? It might be safer –'

'No,' Drake said, cutting across him. 'We're staying here.'

Abby looked back at Tom and shrugged. 'I guess I'm staying. Take Jason, though.'

'No,' Jason begged. 'Mom, I want to stay with you.'

He thought back to the Jason of earlier that day. At first he had thought the storm might be fun. He'd imagined riding it out, safe in his

41

own house, and then going back to school with a great story to tell the other kids. He'd been so sure that he didn't want to go to Grandma's. Now he was having doubts. He was more scared than he had ever been before. He couldn't get that jogger out of his mind. He couldn't stop thinking that, if he went with Tom now and the storm turned out to be as bad as everyone thought, this might be the last time he would see his parents. He would rather stay here and see it out than go away and face that.

'Sure he's staying,' Drake said, interrupting his thoughts. His father never yelled, hardly ever sounded annoyed even, but somehow you didn't argue with him.

Abby shrugged again. Bob and Ellen were already getting back into the truck.

Tom hesitated before he followed them. 'Good luck. I reckon you're going to need it.'

Drake shook hands with him. 'You'll need it more than we will, Tom.'

Abby and Jason just said goodbye.

Tom nodded, looked as if he was about to say something else, and then went back to the truck and hauled himself up into the cab. Ellen waved as he started the engine again and steered the truck in a circle and back down the dirt road.

Jason stood on the veranda until the sound of the engine died away in the wind and the rustling of the trees. Then he braved the rain for as long as it took him to pick up the gas cylinder and carry it through to the kitchen. He heard his father locking up the front door and pushing the bolts into place.

Even though the window shutters were in place, the kitchen seemed no darker than before, but now the storm was loud outside. The wood panels rattled and he heard long, straining groans from all around as the house resisted the ferocious elements outside.

His mother had already brought in the carrier bags and was unpacking them. 'Tiger did well out of this,' she said, stacking the tins of cat food in a cupboard.

'Did he come back?' Jason asked, looking around his feet for a sign that the mad moggy was safely indoors.

His mother shook her head. She was looking upset. 'Jason,' she said slowly, 'we couldn't find him.'

He thought about her words and what they meant. What if Tiger never came back? It wouldn't be like home any more.

'I'm going to go and look,' he said and, before his mother could protest, he added, 'I promised Bethy.'

He went out through the back door. The wind caught it as he turned the door handle and he had to fight to get it closed behind him. He yelled into the churning maelstrom of wind and rain in front of him.

'Tiger! Tiger!'

But he had not really expected the cat to come on his call. Tucking his head in and hunching his shoulders, he ran across the open ground, past the garage and the store for machinery, fighting against the wind and rain, until he reached the first line of orange trees.

'Tiger! Here, kitty, kitty! Food! Come and get it, Tiger!'

He felt he was shouting over the storm. He could hardly hear himself and he did not expect that a cat, hiding wherever a cat would hide, would be able to hear him.

He could see nothing but gusts of rain and thrashing branches. Even so, he stumbled on, a few metres further into the trees, trying to see if Tiger had climbed into one of them. Then he stopped and clutched his head. There were rows upon rows of trees. Did he really expect to find the single one that the cat had chosen to hide in?

Pricking up his ears, he thought he could hear his mother's desperate voice shouting his name. Feeling miserable and wet, and knowing that his search was hopeless, he turned back. He was half carried by the wind now and it flung him against the garage wall. Maybe Tiger had gone in there, Jason thought, but when he tried the door it was locked. So was the door of the machine store; his father must have closed everything up while Jason and Tom had been away. If Tiger was in there, he was as safe as anywhere.

Jason let the wind sweep him back to the house. He slipped on the churned-up mud and his hands sank into the earth as he thrust them out to cushion his fall. Righting himself, he lurched forward.

His mother was watching for him. She opened the back door a crack to let him in; he scrambled through and she slammed it shut again.

Inside, his father rammed home the bolts that they hoped would hold the door against the mounting pressure.

Jason stood in the middle of the floor, gasping. Water was streaming off him and pooling on the floor.

'You don't go out there again, do you hear?' his mother gasped, throwing a towel round his shoulders.

Jason nodded. 'I had to try.'

'OK. It's OK,' his mother soothed him. 'Go

and change into dry clothes.'

As Jason headed upstairs to his bedroom, he could hear her thumping his father on the shoulder and muttering, 'Just like his father . . .'

Jason flicked on his bedroom light. It flickered for a moment and he remembered what his father had said about the possibility of the power lines coming down. He held his breath but, for now at least, the light stayed on.

Shivering, he stripped off his wet clothes, towelled himself dry, and put on jeans and a sweatshirt. The shutters on his window rattled, the wind outside refusing to let him forget the danger that was upon them.

When he came down again, his mother was still in the kitchen, filling a white plastic container with water from the tap.

'Here, Jason, you can do this,' she said. 'Fill them all.'

Jason saw a whole line of containers on the floor by the sink. Two were full already, and he took over the task of filling the third.

'D'you think they'll cut off the water, then?' he asked.

'They might.'

The radio was switched on to the weather reports. Jason realized that the announcer was talking about the rising tide. The voice sounded calm and matter-of-fact, just saying where the tide was likely to be highest, and when, and warning people to stay out of the area.

'Did you say you saw the swell, Jason?' Abby asked.

'Yeah. It was . . . kind of scary.'

'You shouldn't have been anywhere near the coast!' she said, unable to conceal the concern in her voice.

'We weren't, Mom, honest. We were up on that little bluff, you know, near Palm Sands — where you can see right down to the beach. It wasn't dangerous, Mom.'

Outside, the wind read his thoughts and replied. The noise surrounding the house changed. It rose to a howling, and then to a shriek. The house shuddered as if a giant hand had grabbed it. Somewhere outside, in the distance, there was a crash. The shrieking went on.

Drake Mitchell appeared in the kitchen doorway. He looked calm but he was gripping the door frame so tightly that his knuckles were visibly white.

'Well,' he said. 'I guess this is it.'

CHAPTER SIX

Jason sat in the sitting-room with his hands wrapped round a mug of coffee. He sipped the hot drink slowly, occasionally looking up when he heard a particularly loud crash above his head or the howl of the wind. Jason didn't usually drink coffee, but now he felt he needed something warm. Something reassuring.

Drake Mitchell was settled in his favourite chair and had taken out a book. Going past to take a broken biscuit from the plate on the low table beside him, Jason squinted at it to see what it was. Shakespeare? Shakespeare in the middle of a hurricane? Jason shook his head. Sometimes he thought his dad was weird.

'Haven't you anything to do, Jason?' his father asked. 'No assignments for school?'

Jason groaned. He was supposed to sit here, waiting to be blown away, and do history? His dad wasn't just weird, he decided; he was totally out of his tree.

'No, Dad,' he lied.

His father gave Jason a look, as if he didn't believe him, but didn't push it. He just settled back contentedly and got on with his book.

After a few minutes, Abby switched on the TV, and she kept changing channels until she found the weather report. Glittering bands of light kept sweeping over the screen, distorting the picture, and sometimes crackling almost drowned the sound. The storm was interfering with the transmission.

Jason had half expected pictures of the storm, and maybe the damage it had done, but what came up on the screen was a news bulletin from an announcer in the studio. Maybe no one had felt like taking a TV camera outside, Jason thought. He didn't blame them.

Abby had caught the last part of a report about the growing storm. The announcer was talking about the impending hurricane in her usual voice, safe in the knowledge that she was well away from the area it was currently devastating. The extent of the damage and the number of casualties, she said, were still unknown.

After hitting the coast further south, the hurricane was moving north and inland, gaining strength as it went. Winds of over a hundred and fifty kilometres an hour had been reported, before the storm had ripped out the equipment meant to measure it. It was, the announcer said, officially a hurricane and the Hurricane Centre had named it Gordon.

'Gee, we're official. Isn't that great?' Jason muttered, and then he laughed at the irony of the hurricane being called Gordon. His cousin was going to love that. Jason wouldn't hear the end of it until Christmas.

The station was telling everyone who was accidentally stranded in the area to stay put. But what about the ones who *deliberately* stayed, Jason thought. He guessed they thought nobody would have been that stupid. Jason looked at his father, reading his book and pretending to ignore the TV. But then again, they hadn't met Drake Mitchell.

The high winds and heavy rain had made most of the roads too dangerous to travel on. The announcer gave the locations of shelters where people could go to ride out the storm. Jason thought about Tom and hoped that he was OK.

Drake Mitchell snorted, proof that he was listening after all.

'An hour ago,' he said, 'they were telling us all to evacuate. Scare-mongering, just as I said. Maybe now they'll make up their minds.'

Jason knew there was no point in telling his father that the advice had changed because Hurricane Gordon was already upon them, and getting worse. There was nowhere to run to any more. But Drake knew that anyway. He just liked to complain about anybody who tried to tell him what to do.

Then the announcer moved on to a report from the north of the State, where local authorities were trying to cope with the evacuees. Abby left the TV on but turned the sound down, and she got out her sewing box with a nightgown she was embroidering for Bethy.

With the lights on and his parents quietly occupied, Jason thought it might almost be an ordinary evening at home, with Bethy asleep upstairs and Tiger out terrorizing the local wildlife. All that stopped him believing it was the noise of the wind. He was not sure whether to be scared or bored. Maybe his dad had a point, he admitted, about that history. At least it would take his mind off the storm.

But he was not ready to give in and get his books out yet. He wondered whether to go upstairs to his room and play games on his computer, but somehow he didn't want to sit up there by himself. If Bethy was here, he thought, we could play a game. I'd even let her win.

He was wondering if he had a book he felt like reading, when suddenly there was a loud crackle from the TV set, and the screen went blank. At the same moment all the lights went out.

Abby muttered something, and Drake said calmly, 'There go the power lines.'

Jason tried to peer into the darkness. He couldn't see anything, though he did hear movement coming from the direction of his father. Then the room was dimly lit again as Drake snapped on a torch.

Abby put her sewing aside and said, sounding irritated but not particularly worried, 'I'll have to cook dinner on the camping stove. Something out of the freezer, I guess. All that stuff's going to spoil now. What about frozen paella, Jason, and all the pecan nut ice-cream you can eat?'

'Yeah, great,' Jason said flatly.

Not knowing why, he got up, went over to the phone and picked up the receiver. It was dead. 'Phone's out, too,' he said.

'Then your Grandma can't call us to tell us all how stupid we're being,' Drake said, the torchlight revealing his wry smile.

'Fetch the radio from the kitchen, will you, Jason?' Abby asked.

When Jason came back with the radio, he spent the first few minutes trying to tune it to the citizens' band. Not much more than static was getting through. Then he picked up a report about how the State Governor had suspended the tolls on the turnpike to speed up traffic flow, and had declared a state of emergency, with the National Guard ready to move in. The voices came through clearly at first, but gradually faded and then were lost in another wash of static.

'I guess it's the batteries,' Jason said unconvincingly, and he flicked it off.

In the dim light, with nothing coming from the television or radio, the wind sounded louder. Jason was suddenly doubly aware of all the little creaks and scraping noises coming from the house itself. From outside, as well as the shrieking wind, he could hear a distant rumbling and crashing and then, close up and even louder, a thud, as if something had hit the side of the house.

Jason went over to the window and tried to peer out through a crack in the shutters, but they fitted tightly. All he could see, with one eye pressed against the thin opening, was a grey-green, swirling mass, as if the whole citrus grove was on the move, dancing wildly round the house.

'I've got some candles.'

Jason peeled his eye off the window. His mother was framed in the doorway, holding out some long, white, wax candles.

Jason gave her a hand, and together they illuminated the room with flickering light.

Suddenly, a drawn-out splintering sound echoed round the room. Everyone snapped to attention. A wide chunk of dull light flooded into the room as one of the window shutters was torn away.

'Oh, my,' Abby said, clutching Jason's arm tightly.

The splintering noise returned, as the second shutter followed the first.

Jason hunched his shoulders, expecting the window to break, but for the time being it held.

He could see outside for the first time since the storm had got really bad. The air was dark. One of the posts at the front of the veranda had been ripped away, and the corner of the roof was sagging. At a distance, the orange trees lashed back and forth as if they were trying to pull up their own roots. Rain was whipping straight past the window. A bright red garden chair – not one of theirs, Jason realized – sailed across their view at tree-top height and vanished. Green lightning crackled across the sky.

Drake got up and left the room. First he went into the kitchen, then to the dining-room, and finally upstairs. Jason and Abby listened to him moving about. He came back, looking satisfied.

'All safe so far,' he said gruffly. 'Jason, why don't you –'

Jason never found out what his father wanted him to do. He broke off as his words were drowned out by the loudest noise yet – a crashing and tearing that came from directly above their heads, followed by a whole series of bangs and thumps on the ceiling. Several uneven chunks of plaster over the chair where Drake had been sitting crashed to the floor in one corner.

Jason's father turned around as if he meant to go back upstairs.

'Drake! Don't go up there!' Abby screamed.

For once Drake did as he was told. He stood, looking up at the ceiling as if he could see through it and find out what was happening.

Jason peered out of the window. Everything was so confusing. There seemed to be more dust and debris in the air, and what he thought were leaves or feathers being swirled around in the wind.

A whole section of board flapped into view like the wing of an enormous bird. It swooped down on the open space in front of the house and then took off again, and was flung into the trees, disintegrating as it went. The feathers, Jason realized, were not feathers at all, but shingles from the roof.

'That's our roof!' Jason yelled. 'Mom, Dad, our roof just blew away!'

CHAPTER SEVEN

'**M**y colonial chest!' Abby Mitchell cried. 'Great–Grandma's patchwork quilt!'

And my computer, Jason thought. Rain and the debris from the roof were really going to mess it up, although if the storm kept on much longer he'd probably have to follow it into the next State to find out what the damage was.

He heard his mother gasp. He spun around. His parents were looking up at the ceiling. It was sagging in the middle. A network of cracks had spread across it. Water began to trickle down on to their heads.

'What are we going to do?' Jason said desperately.

'There's not much we *can* do,' Drake said.

'We've got to sit it out.'

'But for how much longer, Drake?' Abby pleaded.

No one answered, and she did not seem to expect a reply. She went out to the kitchen and came back a few minutes later with an armful of bowls and buckets to put under the worst of the drips.

Jason went to help her, though he felt it wasn't much use. Then he realized that he could hear the sound of water pattering into the buckets. The wind had dropped. The noise was dying away. The rattling had stopped. He went to join his father, who was looking out of the window. Across the open space, the orange trees were waving gently. Leaves drifted down and lightly covered the debris that was already littering the floor outside.

'This must be the eye,' Drake said, letting out a short sigh. 'Well, it could be worse, I guess.'

'Could be worse?' Abby said. She slammed down the last bucket and came over to the window. 'No phone, no electricity and no roof, and you say it could be worse?'

Drake grinned. His worried look had gone.

'We're still here,' he said. 'So far.' He strode across to the door and opened it. 'I'm going to take a look outside. We won't have long. I want to see what the damage is. Jason, come with me.'

Instinctively, Jason followed his father on to the veranda. Most of it was still intact, though three of the posts and the steps had gone, and the morning glories hung, tattered, on the trellis. Drake jumped down and walked backwards away from the house, looking up at the roof. Jason ran after him, picking his way through the debris.

The roof straps that should have protected the house were gone. Over half the roof had been ripped away and the walls were sticking up like jagged teeth. The part that remained looked as if it had shifted and could be hanging on by just a few nails.

Drake snorted but said nothing. He set off round the side of the house, towards the garage and the machine store. For a minute, Jason stayed where he was, looking around.

The orderly rows of citrus were broken up now, with gaps clearly visible – in other places trees leant awkwardly at a drunken angle. Only a light breeze stirred the leaves that still clung to them. Fruit was scattered on the ground beneath.

Jason could still hear the storm wind, as if it was blowing at a distance; immediately around the house, however, the air was almost completely still, and it felt almost as hot and sticky as it had done at school that morning.

Jason shuffled his feet. He could have expected to feel relieved when the wind dropped, but he didn't. The distant sound of the storm, the heavy air – they were too spooky. The eye of the hurricane – the quiet place in the middle of the storm – made him more uneasy than the storm itself. He wondered how much longer it would be before the wind got up again.

His mother appeared in the doorway. 'Jason, where's your father?'

'Round the back. Do you want him?'

'No, you'll do. Come and help me move this chest downstairs.' Her voice sounded urgent.

Jason peered after his father but couldn't see him, so he went back into the house and followed his mother upstairs and into his parents' bedroom, now completely open to the sky. There were chairs tipped over, and everything on the dressing table had been swept off and smashed. Apart from rain soaking everything and puddles on the rug, there wasn't a lot of damage. The room just looked as if someone had given it a good shake.

He picked up one end of his mother's precious antique chest while she took the other, and they manoeuvred it downstairs and into the dining-room. Jason saw that his mother had already moved some stuff; Great-Grandma's patchwork quilt was rolled up next to some photograph albums and a model dinosaur he'd made in first grade. He grinned; Mom had a weird collection of treasures!

When he had helped her put the chest where she wanted it, he went back upstairs to his own room. Most of his ceiling was still intact, though there was a gaping hole in one corner, and leaves and all kinds of stuff had blown through it, along with the rain.

He mopped his computer with the T-shirt he'd left lying there earlier, and started to carry it downstairs. On the way he heard his father calling him. 'Coming, Dad!'

He left the computer on the dining-room table and went outside again. Drake had reappeared from the back of the house.

'Jason, don't keep wandering off,' he said. 'I want you to help me move the big ladder. Quickly, we're running out of time.'

'I was helping Mom . . .' Jason started to protest, but Drake wasn't listening, and he followed him to the machine store.

The store and the garage were both part of a single low building, at right angles to the house. It looked undamaged. Drake had unlocked the door, and he and Jason moved out the longest ladder and set it up against the side of the house.

'There's some rolls of canvas in here,' Drake said. 'I want to cover up the hole in the roof with it before the wind gets up again.'

Jason looked up at the sky. It was almost clear overhead, though he could see dark clouds in the distance, and he could still hear the distant roaring of the wind.

'I don't like this, Dad,' he said. 'It's . . . kind of weird.'

Drake shrugged. He had started to hum a cheerful tune as he went back to fetch the canvas.

Jason went to help. In the machine store, he could not help poking about in the corners, wondering if Tiger had taken shelter there.

'Jason, what are you doing?' his father asked irritably.

'Looking for Tiger.'

'Oh.' Drake's irritation suddenly vanished. 'Yes, I know. It's tough.'

Jason scuffed his feet. 'I just thought he might have come in here.'

Again, Jason knew it was a false hope. If Tiger had been stuck in here all through the storm, as soon as his father opened the door he would have been bowled over by a yowling bundle of infuriated striped fur. Tiger wouldn't be cowering away in a corner.

'What're we going to tell Bethy?' Jason asked.

'I'll buy her another kitten.'

Drake didn't sound happy about it. 'Another kitten' wouldn't do. He looked angry – not with Jason, or Bethy, or even with Tiger – he was angry with the world for not being how he wanted it to be. That was just like his dad, Jason thought. He even wanted the wind to blow to order.

Drake picked up the end of a roll of canvas and started to drag it out. Jason picked up the other end, and they carried it to where they had left the ladder.

'Go and fetch me the old leather gardening gloves from the kitchen,' Drake said. 'And ask your Mom if she can manage coffee. Oh, and Jason – tell her to unplug all the electrical stuff. If the power comes back, with all this water someone could be electrocuted.'

Jason did as he was told and relayed the messages. His mother already had a pot of water heating on the camping stove.

'Tell him I'll make dinner pretty soon,' she said. 'I'll do it before it gets dark. I guess we won't have the electricity back today.'

Jason went out on to the veranda again with

the gloves. As soon as he stepped outside, he could feel how the air had changed. It had been warm and clammy; he had felt too hot in his sweatshirt. Now it was chilly again. Clouds were racing across the sky, covering up the vivid blue. Rain suddenly began spattering down and grew heavier with every drop.

'Dad?' Jason called out, with uncertainty.

With a deafening roar, the wind struck. Jason felt it clutch him and drive him along the veranda, his feet hardly touching the ground. He grabbed at the trellis, and it broke away; he grabbed again, and this time managed to stop himself before he was swept away from the house.

'Dad!' he yelled into the gale.

The air was closing in and the light was melting away. Through whirling dust Jason glimpsed the ladder; his father was clinging to it, about half way up. Then the ladder swung out a massive distance away from the side of the house and hit the ground. Grit stung Jason's eyes; he blinked away tears. When his sight cleared, he could see the ladder again, almost upright and pirouetting into the trees like a mad dancer. His father was gone.

CHAPTER EIGHT

'**D**ad!' Jason yelled. 'Dad!'
The wind screamed back in his face.
It was like a huge hand, grabbing at him. He
clung to the splintered trellis and peered out
across the veranda. The air was a churning
soup of dirt and debris; rain lashed at him,
pouring from a dark sky. There was no sign of
his father.

'Jason!' His mother's voice was near. He
turned to see her holding on to the door
frame. 'Jason, get back in here! Please!'

The doorway was two or three metres away.
Jason wanted to dive through it, into the safety
of the house, but he dared not let go of the
trellis. If he did, the wind would take him. He
could see himself tossed in it, struggling,

carried up and away, until it got tired of him and smashed him to the ground.

'I can't!' he shouted.

Keeping a grip on the door frame, Abby Mitchell stepped out on to the veranda. The wind slapped her against the side of the house. She stretched out a hand to Jason. He strained towards her, but he couldn't reach.

'I can't!' he repeated.

There was a creaking sound, tiny beside the shrieking wind, but very close. The trellis Jason was hanging on to was slowly tearing away from the wall.

'Jason!' his mother screamed.

Desperately he threw himself across the gap, clutching blindly, and felt his mother's fingers fasten round his wrist. For a moment they swayed with the wind all round them, and then, in a rush, they fell back together inside.

Jason knelt there, gasping. He could hear the storm, but the air round him was still. He looked up to see his mother leaning back against the bolted door.

'Mom, he's gone,' he whimpered. 'Dad's gone.'

Abby leant forward. Her hair had fallen round her shoulders and blood was trickling from a scratch on her forehead. For a minute

Jason thought she was going to start crying. He could see her fighting it.

'Mom, what are we going to do?' he asked.

'Do? There's nothing we can do.' His mother's voice came out quite steadily. 'Your father can look after himself.'

She held out a hand to haul Jason up off the floor.

'In that?' Jason's voice rose. He kept twisting around, trying to face his mother as she pushed him through the door into the sitting-room. 'I'm not a kid, Mom. He's dead, isn't he? He's bound to be dead if he's out there in that.'

Abby swallowed. Her voice quivered. 'Maybe. But we don't know. We can't know until –'

She broke off as another blast hit the house. Something burst through the window. Instinctively Jason crouched, wrapping his arms round his head against the spraying glass. Storm billowed into the room.

Abby grabbed Jason and shoved him across the floor into the sheltered space between the sofa and the wall. The house was groaning round them. The wind was inside with them now, raging. The water buckets catching rainwater tipped and spilt their load. Chairs crashed over, and the side-table where Abby always kept a bowl of flowers spilled over. The bowl shattered; the flowers danced in the air. His father's books were tossed back and forth, pages fluttering. The coffee mugs they had used earlier were hurled at the wall. One of them struck the television screen and smashed the glass.

All Jason wanted to do was lie still and forget everything. He'd had enough. His father was somewhere out there. Drake Mitchell. Tough, irritable, and as stubborn as a whole herd of mules. Too stubborn to leave. He'd got Mom and him into this, and now he was probably dead.

Upstairs, something crashed over. The ceiling shook. Bits of plaster rained down. From above came a long, dragging sound, as if a heavy weight was being pushed across the floor. There was the sound of more loud splintering. One corner of the ceiling sagged and water poured down through the new holes.

'Mom, the house is breaking up!' Jason wailed. He was really scared now.

Abby was tightly calm. She sat with her back against the wall, her knees drawn up to her chin and her arms clasped round them.

'We can only wait it out,' she said. 'Hope the house holds. Like your father said.'

Jason sat up and leant against the wall beside her. 'Maybe Dad's OK.'

His mother gave him a faint smile. Neither of them believed it.

The roaring of the storm had risen so that Jason could not make out separate noises, nor could he guess what any of it meant. The whole world was howling and banging round him. The ground vibrated. He clamped his hands over his ears, but that was not enough to shut it out. The noise seeped between his fingers.

The room was shivering, tugging at the ground like a gas balloon that wanted to be free. The floor tilted. Furniture shifted. The last upright chair rocked and tipped over. The big old sofa rolled a short distance until it got stuck in the rucked-up rug.

Then, even the grey storm light was blotted out as what looked like a whole tree flapped against the window frame and clung there like a monstrous green bird. The house shuddered under the impact.

Light poured in again – a gaping mouth of light, as one whole wall tore away from its struts and braces, swung back and forth as if it was on hinges, and was whipped out of sight. Rain swirled in. The ceiling began to break apart. A second wall peeled away like orange rind.

Yelling furiously, Jason tried to stand up, but

the wind caught him and rolled him over. He hit something, made a grab for it, and was carried on. Pain lanced up one leg. He thrashed helplessly at the air as he felt himself being lifted and flung out into the boiling mass of the storm.

Then he was lying, face down, with grass under his hands. He tried to dig his fingers into the soil. He could taste dirt in his mouth. Grit stung his eyes; he was breathing it, choking on it. Rain hammered down on his unprotected back.

Something slammed into him; he started fighting it off, until he heard his mother's voice gasping, 'Jason!' into his ear. She was lying half on top of him, one arm braced round his shoulders. Then the wind took both of them and dragged them along the ground. Grit pricked his fingertips as he desperately scrabbled at the earth for a grip.

A splintered tree-stump swam out of the darkness. Jason lunged at it. Spikes of wood drove into his hand, but the wind ripped him away, half lifted him, then threw him against something hard with a blow that made his head ring and drove all the breath out of him.

Coughing, he fought for air. He could see nothing but the whirling dark. Then, as his head cleared, he realized he was not being carried along any more. He was lying against a tree. It certainly felt like a tree – he still couldn't see. His mother had one arm locked round the trunk and the other still gripped his shoulders.

The wind wrenched at them. Jason groped for the trunk, got his hands to it and his arms round it, hugging it with all his strength. Muzzily, he realized it was one of his father's orange trees. It bent and swayed in the storm.

If this goes, Jason thought, we're dead.

'Hang on, Jason. Just hang on.' His mother was screaming in his ear, but it sounded like a whisper.

Jason never knew how long they spent lying there, clinging to the orange tree and to each other. Time stretched like elastic. There had never been anything before this howling darkness. There would never be anything afterwards.

All kinds of weird thoughts were tumbling through his brain. Distant memories flooded back, overloading his senses – like having to squint when looking through a brightly lit window: the day he made the baseball team; driving to the beach with his mum and Gordon; his dad grinning delightedly as Bethy took her first, unsteady steps.

He wanted to close his eyes, but he couldn't. His situation jammed them open. He was still sprawled on the ground, battered by stinging rain and debris. His leg throbbed with pain. His arms felt numb, and he wasn't sure whether or not they had already been yanked off.

Then, gradually, he realized that the storm was dying. Daylight was growing again. He could see further than the tree trunk and the patch of earth round it. The rain was easing off; it was hurting less. Jason stopped feeling that the wind was tugging him away, but it was a long time before he could relax his arms, still clamped round the tree.

At last Abby let out a long sigh, let go her grip on him, and sat up. 'Are you hurt?' she said. Her voice was drained and weak.

Jason pushed himself up on to one elbow. There was a long, nagging ache down his leg, and one hand was stuck full of splinters. He quickly pulled out the worst and sucked the heel of his hand where it was bleeding.

'I guess I'm OK,' he said. He used the tree to pull himself upright, then he flexed the painful leg at knee and ankle. His jeans were torn, and blood was oozing sluggishly from a ragged gash, but all the bits seemed to work. 'I guess so,' he repeated, wobbling slightly.

Abby stood up and looked around. She

seemed uninjured, too, except for scratches on her face and hands, and a bruise already starting to darken one side of her face.

They had, Jason realized, been incredibly lucky.

His sodden clothes were clinging to him clammily, and he tried without much success to squeeze water out of his sweatshirt. All around he could hear soft creaking noises and the sound of a light wind rustling through the surviving trees. Rain pattered from the leaves on to ground awash with puddles. Above his head the clouds were thinning out.

The storm was over. The straight lines of orange trees had been broken up, like an army under enemy fire. Some trees were torn up and lay with their roots writhing in the air. Some were just gone, leaving either shattered stumps or nothing but a scar on the earth. Others still stood, wreckage hanging in their branches.

Abby started to pick her way through the trees, back towards the house. Jason followed, splashing and slipping on the swampy ground. Before he left the tree they had held on to – the tree that had saved their lives – he gave its trunk a little pat. 'Thanks, pal.'

Blood was still trickling from his hand, so he fished out a handkerchief and pressed it against his palm.

'I need a Band-Aid,' he said.

'You'll have to find the first-aid kit first,' Abby replied, without looking back. 'Or rather,' she added as she came to a halt at the edge of the trees, 'you'll have to find the house first.'

Jason came to her side and stared. Where the house had been, only one whole wall was standing, and part of a second. He could see a section of the staircase and a metre or so of the upper floor jutting out into empty air. Water pipes and wiring were twisted like creepers. The bathtub had crashed down and looked as if it was trying to burrow through the foundations. Smashed furniture was piled everywhere.

'Mom!' he gasped.

Abby was standing very still. She had a strange look on her face, a look Jason had only seen once or twice before, when she had been really, *seriously* angry. She took a deep breath. 'It's getting late,' she said. Her voice sounded just like always. 'Dark, too, in a couple of hours, I guess. Don't stand there gaping, Jason, there's a lot to do. It isn't over yet.'

Jason had automatically looked at his watch when his mother mentioned the time, but it was smashed. Somehow that tiny detail told him that it really *wasn't* all over. The hurricane

74

had moved on, but they still had problems. Big problems. They still had to cope with the damage.

They had no home any more.

They didn't have a bed for the night.

There was no food – and no way of cooking it if they had.

They couldn't even drive into town for a pizza. Jason felt hungry. His leg hurt, and his hand hurt, and he was more tired than he had ever been in his life. He wanted to flop down somewhere and rest, but he guessed he wouldn't be getting any rest for a long time.

Abby must have been thinking along the same lines.

'We need shelter,' she said, 'before it gets dark tonight. And something to eat. And some sort of signal to tell the rescue services we're here. I'll get started on that.'

She paused and then added, 'Jason, I want you to start looking for your father.'

CHAPTER NINE

Without waiting for any reply from Jason, Abby strode off purposefully towards the wreck of the house. Jason stared after her. He didn't *want* to look for his father. He didn't want to look and not find him, and not know what had happened to him. At the same time, he was afraid of looking and finding his father dead.

But his mother was right. She was the best person to start bringing some sort of order back into the mess their lives had suddenly become. That left just one job for Jason.

'Well,' he muttered to himself, 'you're not a kid any more, Jase.'

He bent down and bound his handkerchief round the gash in his leg, then straightened up and looked around. He could remember, just about, the place where the ladder had disappeared into the trees. His father hadn't been carried along with it, but at least that was the right direction. It was a place to start.

Jason turned back into the trees. He was shivering. There was still some wind and, now and then, a gust of rain. The trees looked as if they were shivering with him. Nearly all their leaves had been stripped off, but Jason was surprised to see that most of the fruit was still clinging to the branches. What sort of wind was it that could blow his house away but still leave the fruit on the trees?

He stopped and rubbed his hands over his face. This was stupid. He was thinking these thoughts so that he didn't have to think about his father. He went on, looking around more carefully now.

Wreckage was strewn all around and was even caught up in the trees. Jason stepped over what looked like a section of the roof. There was a chair, set upright beneath a tree, as if someone had felt like sitting outside to enjoy the fresh air. The tree beside it had a plank driven sideways through its trunk. Another was swathed in something glittery, and after a moment Jason recognized it as what was left of his mother's best evening dress.

A few metres further along, he found the ice-box, hanging upside down in a tree, with its flex dangling. The door was closed. Without thinking, Jason reached up and yanked it open.

Food rained down on him. He ducked his head and let it bounce off. Cartons of milk and orange juice. A can of Coke. That hurt. Cheese and pepperoni and butter and half a watermelon followed. A plastic bowl of salad that scattered across the ground.

Jason gathered up the items that were still fit to eat and made his way, his arms full, back towards the house.

Mom should be pleased, he thought. Then he remembered that this wasn't what he had been sent to do.

When Jason got back to the remains of the house, Abby was picking her way through the debris with a blanket bundled up in her arms. She started to spread it out to dry over part of the splintered wall, but she stopped as she saw Jason.

'Well?' she said, looking straight at him.

Her voice was sharp. Jason could tell how worried she was, though she was trying not to show it.

'I haven't found him, Mom,' he replied, almost apologetically. 'But I found the ice-box.'

He put the food down on a clear patch of ground.

Abby stared at it for a minute as if she wasn't sure what it was, then she shook herself. 'Good. That'll do fine, Jason. Just carry on.'

Part of him, Jason admitted to himself, had been hoping she might say he needn't go on looking. But he knew that she wouldn't. He had to keep trying. There was no one else to do it. While Abby went on spreading out the blanket to dry, he went back towards the trees.

He tried calling, 'Dad! Dad!' a few times, but there was no reply. Did he really expect one? Even if Drake Mitchell was still alive, he might not be where he could hear. He might not be able to reply.

Jason remembered how he had looked for Tiger, earlier in the day. This was just the same, wandering through the trees and calling, and realizing just how many trees there were, and how small in comparison the person was that he was looking for.

He stopped and leant against one of the trees. The search wasn't any good. He was only one person, and the area was too big to cover. Think, then, he said to himself. Think, and try to cut it down. He remembered how he and his mother had survived by hanging on to a tree. You *didn't* have to die if you were out in the storm; he'd proved that. He pushed away the thought that his father had been out in the turmoil for much longer. If it was possible to survive, then Drake Mitchell would have done it. He was that sort of man.

Right, Jason reasoned. Dad's alive. But hurt somehow. If he wasn't hurt, he would be striding round the place by now, telling everyone what to do. So where is he? What would he have done if he found himself out in the storm?

The only answer Jason could come up with was that his father would have hung on to something, just as they had, so that the wind couldn't carry him away. Jason tried to picture his father clinging to a tree. Sure, but was that all? If Drake Mitchell had thought he could do more to protect himself, what would he have done? The answer to that came very easily. He would have tried to get back to the house. To us.

Slowly Jason retraced his steps. He was still amazed at the wreckage that festooned the trees or was piled up on the ground: Their smashed TV set had been slammed into the earth and half buried; next, Jason came upon a usable bucket and he picked it up almost without thinking; strangest of all, there was a small boat, upside down and apparently undamaged, as if the tide had just washed it up and left it.

Jason bent down and heaved the boat up so that he could peer under it. He was partly afraid of seeing his father's twitching body, partly hoping that Tiger might come shooting out – but neither was there.

He straightened up again, and his stomach lurched as he saw, beyond the boat, a humped shape swathed in plastic sheeting. A shape the right size for a huddled body, lying very still.

Breathing hard, Jason walked up to it. He grabbed one edge of the sheeting and gave it a jerk, squeezing his eyes shut as he did so. When he dared to open them again, he almost collapsed into uncontrolled nervous laughter. The 'body' was no more than an untidy tangle of rope.

Jason clenched his teeth against the laughter and went on, skirting round a patch of ground that bristled with smashed china and glass. As his breathing grew steadier, he kept on looking, but he had the feeling that he was not going to find anything here.

Back at the house, he left the bucket and shook his head in reply to the look his mother gave him. He had an idea. The garage and machine store behind the house – or where the house had been – had survived better than the house itself. The roof and one door had been ripped off, but most of the walls still stood.

Jason had helped his father to carry out the ladder and the canvas just before the hurricane returned. They had left the door swinging open behind them.

He squelched across the grass to the gap where the door had been. The storm had been in there all right. The machinery was all churned up together, as if somebody had put it all in an enormous bowl and stirred it. The partition between the store and the garage was broken down. His father's station wagon had been flipped over on to its roof, and it lay, canted on the pile of machinery, with its wheels in the air like a stranded beetle. His mother's little runabout was smashed against it.

'Dad?' Jason whispered tentatively into the mêlée.

There was no reply – he had not expected one – but something told Jason not to turn away. He let his eyes scan the mass of wreckage, from side to side and top to bottom. At first he thought there was nothing but twisted metal, but then his eyes focused on something that stirred his heart.

His pulse quickened. There was something small, very small but familiar, sticking out from underneath the wrecked cars. A foot. Just one foot, shod in a blue sneaker. Exactly like the ones his father had been wearing.

CHAPTER TEN

Jason drew back from the doorway. For a moment the world spun round him as if the wind was still blowing. He took a deep breath, and his vision cleared.

He looked towards the house and yelled, 'Mom!'

Abby appeared from behind the remains of the house.

'Mom!' he cried again.

When Abby reached the doorway, Jason could do nothing but point. His mother stood, simply looking for a minute without saying anything. He had no idea what she was already thinking about the fate of her husband. Then she stepped forward and started to circle slowly round the heap of twisted metal, and suddenly she seemed to plunge into it on hands and knees. Something shifted, settled; there was a grinding sound.

'Mom!' Jason said, terrified.

The movement stopped. Soon Abby reappeared, backing out more slowly. Her face was flushed and her eyes bright.

'Sorry,' she said apologetically. 'Didn't mean to scare you. Jason, he's alive.'

'Alive?' Jason repeated. For a moment he could hardly understand what that meant. It had been an impossible thought that Jason had already spent an hour steeling himself against. 'How . . . How can he be alive, under all that?'

His mother beckoned to him. 'Come round here, round the edge. Careful. Don't touch anything.'

When he had picked his way round to where his mother was standing, he could see into a kind of little cave on the garage floor, created artificially where one car had been forced up against the other. He could see his father's head and shoulders, and one arm flung out. From the waist down, he was trapped under the cars. His head was turned away and he was not moving.

'I felt his pulse,' Abby said. 'And his head looks OK. I guess his legs must be broken, though.' She sounded calm, but her voice was tight.

'Mom, we've got to get him out of there!' Jason stammered, the possibility that everything might just be all right after all taking hold of his actions and motivations.

He reached out, but Abby grabbed his arm.

'I said, don't touch anything. It's balanced. You saw it shift when I went under there. We could bring the whole lot down on top of him.'

'What are we going to do then?'

Abby motioned him towards the doorway, and together they edged round the cars and got outside. 'We'll need help to get the cars off him. And medical attention. And we need it soon. We can't wait for the phone to be fixed or the rescue services to find us. That'll all take too long. '

Jason swallowed. He knew what was coming next. 'You want me to go into town, Mom?'

His mother smiled at him. 'Yes, Jason. I know it's tough, but it's best if I stay here. I know some first aid. I'll keep him warm and do what I can if he wakes up while you're away. OK?'

Jason nodded. 'OK.'

He didn't like the idea of having to make his way into town through all the wreckage of the storm, but he wouldn't want to trade places with his mother, either. He had no idea what to do for his father. Besides, no one had to tell him that, if help didn't come quickly, his father would die. Jason didn't want to be alone with him if that happened.

'Look out for a working phone,' Abby reminded him. 'Or if you can't find one, go on into town. There'll be a disaster centre someplace, with rescue teams. Find somebody and tell them what we need.'

As she spoke, she was walking with Jason towards the place where the dirt road led off into the trees. She stopped by the little heap of food Jason had brought from the ice-box.

'Best take something,' she said.

Jason managed a weak smile. 'Cheese and pepperoni sandwich, hold the bread.'

Abby thrust the packets into his hands, along with a carton of milk. Then she gave him a long hug. Jason had thought that he was too old for all that stuff, but now he was glad she did, and he hugged her back.

'I won't be long, Mom,' he said, finally letting go of her.

He turned and set off down the dirt road. When he glanced back over his shoulder, his mother was already on her way back to the garage to be with his father.

★

Normally, driving down the dirt road to join the freeway took just a few minutes. Jason couldn't remember the last time when he'd actually walked it on foot.

For the first twenty metres or so it was clear, but then he had to start scrambling over branches and fallen trees. It was going to take a lot longer to reach town, or even a phone, than he'd thought.

The food in his hands got in his way when he had to climb. He managed to stuff the cheese and pepperoni into his jeans pockets, but there was nothing he could do with the milk. He was tempted to drink it and throw the carton away, but he realized that there might come a time when he would need it more than he did now.

While he was searching for his father he had forgotten about the time. The reddening sky above reminded him that the sun was setting. For a minute he stopped, his heart thumping at the thought of trying to force his way through the trees at night, and of being alone in the dark.

'You're not a kid any more,' he muttered to himself again. 'Nobody else can do this.'

He quickened his pace, but following the dirt road was a struggle, and he was already tired. His hands were scratched and his leg still ached. After a while his way was blocked by a whole mass of uprooted trees, tangled together in an impassable mat of trunks and branches. He had to leave the road.

As soon as he stopped trying to move in a straight line, he found it a lot easier to keep going, weaving his way through the gaps in the trees. For the first time Jason wondered if following the road was the most sensible way of going about this. He had automatically taken the route he knew, but was there a better one?

Squatting down, he took a twig and drew a sketch map – as accurately as he could remember – on the ground. The citrus grove; the dirt road; the freeway; the town. Another line for the coast. Looking at it, Jason saw that if he cut through the trees, keeping as near due east as he could manage, sooner or later he would come out into the more open country near the beach, just north of the town. Although trees and cloud prevented him seeing the sun, he could be sure he was moving east if he kept the red glow at his back.

Until it gets dark, something inside his head told him – but he wasn't listening to that voice right now.

Feeling better for the short rest, he moved on, finding the easiest way through the trees. He was still passing all kinds of weird wreckage dangling from the branches like fruit, but he had stopped looking. Speed was what mattered now.

Sometimes he needed to turn away from the east, if uprooted trees or large pieces of wreckage made him take a detour, but he always returned to the line of the setting sun.

At first the glow grew brighter, throwing Jason's shadow in front of him, but eventually it began to fade. Jason's own image was lost among the shadows of the trees. Before very long he had to admit that he could no longer be sure that he was moving in the right direction.

By now he had left the orange trees behind; he must have left his father's land too, although the boundary fence had disappeared in the storm. There was a mixture of various trees round him now, pine and hickory and oak, and undergrowth hiding the ground. His pace slowed again. Sometimes he would stumble into a hole; sometimes the hole had water in it. He listened to himself splashing and crashing along, and he did not know whether to hope someone would hear him, or that they wouldn't.

It would be more sensible, he knew, to stop and rest before it grew too dark. He could have something to eat; he was truly ravenous by now. And later, maybe the moon would be bright enough for him to go on. He tried to remember where the moon would rise, but thick cloud had hidden it the night before. Jason was not even sure whether it would be full enough to give him any useful light.

He came to a halt but, instead of silence as his own footsteps ceased, he heard movement in the undergrowth just ahead of him. His stomach lurched and he froze, listening to the approaching sound: stems breaking, leaves rustling.

There was something out there. Something big.

Jason peered ahead into the dusk. He saw the outlines of the trees in front of him, and on the ground something darker and more solid than the plants round it. At first he couldn't make out what it was. Then a shape lifted up – a silhouette in the twilight. A long, thin, tapering body with stumpy legs moving towards him as if on hinges.

Jason realized he was looking at an alligator.

CHAPTER ELEVEN

Jason swallowed. His legs felt like stone. In the poor light he couldn't see the alligator's eyes, but he had the nasty feeling that it was looking straight at him. A shiny set of razor-sharp teeth glinted in its yawning jaws. He was scared to stay where he was, but he was even more scared to move.

As panic washed through him, he wondered what the creature was doing here. There were no wild alligators in this part of the State. Then he remembered that there was an alligator farm not far away, a place called Great Gators that put on shows for tourists. It must be from there. Maybe their fences and enclosures had been blown away in the hurricane, and this particular brute had escaped.

Jason felt sick. If he was right, then others would have escaped too. The place could be crawling with the things.

The alligator closed its jaws again. Otherwise it had not moved.

Jason tried to stay still. He'd already been holding his pose for what seemed like an eternity, and he wasn't sure how much longer he could avoid twitching. His left foot was slowly sinking into the mud. His hands and fingers were frozen at awkward angles and he felt a desperate need to flex them. Sweat from his forehead trickled down his face and into his eyes. He wanted so much to lift an arm and wipe his eyes clean. But he knew he couldn't.

Jason's mind raced. He remembered visiting Great Gators with Mum and Dad and Bethy. He recalled how quiet the alligators had been, lying in the sun and basking on the edge of the muddy pools. Bethy had wanted to stroke one.

They were big and lazy and awkward, but they had lots of teeth. Their jaws snapped together fast enough. The booklet Abby had bought said they could move quickly over short distances. Great, Jason thought. A short distance was just what separated him from this alligator.

He knew for a certainty that he could not stand there all night and wait for the creature to simply slip away. If the alligator had escaped –

it must be hungry. If it was looking at him, perhaps it was already licking its lips and thinking of its supper. He *had* to move first.

Without turning his head, Jason glanced from side to side. A metre or two away, to his right, was a pine tree with a low branch that stretched out in his direction. Without letting himself think, Jason leapt up – the mud giving up his foot with a loud squelch – and grabbed the branch.

He swung and hauled himself upwards. Below, something heavy splashed along the wet ground. Jason scrabbled for a higher branch, denying huge jaws the opportunity to close over his feet. Clawing and panting, he gained height and at last found himself a safe seat in the fork made by a branch and the thick tree trunk.

For a minute he could do nothing but shiver and catch his breath. When he peered down at the ground, he could see nothing of the alligator, but by now it was so dark that he could not see much of anything. He leant back against the tree trunk and tried to think.

His father was trapped, badly hurt and probably dying. It was Jason's job to get help. If he ever had to concentrate, work hard and successfully complete just one task that his mother asked him to – it was this.

But now he was trapped in this tree. Down

below, there was at least one alligator – maybe more – and if Jason tried to move he could end up as the main course on their dinner menu. If he stayed put, his dad might die.

Despite his pure intentions, Jason felt his body tell him that, for tonight, enough was enough. He needed rest. His limbs ached and the darkening night was inviting sleep. The tree wasn't all that comfortable, but it would do. And he could eat something. He had dropped the carton of milk in his mad scramble into the tree, but he still had the cheese and pepperoni in his pockets – squashed, sure, but Jason wasn't about to complain.

He ate slowly, wondering if he ought to keep some back for later. However, before he knew it, he'd already finished both packs.

With his hunger temporarily dealt with, he realized just how tired he was. It had been a pretty average day when he had got up that morning but, since then, he felt as if he had lived an entire lifetime. He'd plundered every energy store his body held, and it was time to give something back – time to replenish his reserves.

Jason dozed uncomfortably with his back against the rough bark of the tree, one arm hooked round another branch so that he wouldn't fall.

The darkness of sleep finally reclaimed him.

A silvery light shone down into Jason's half-closed eyes and suddenly he jerked awake. The darkness had lifted, the moon was up, and the twisted trees all round him cast eerie grey shadows across the uneven ground.

Jason instantly cocked his head and peered downwards. There was no sign of the alligator, though there were plenty of dark places where it could still be lurking. How long had he been asleep? Minutes or hours? It certainly wasn't enough, and his body screamed its agreement when he tried to flex his limbs.

Jason shook the lingering weariness from his head. He wasn't sure if it was safe to go on. But he knew he had to move.

At the foot of the tree, he looked around again. Nothing. There were no sounds except those he made himself. The milk carton was still there, undamaged, preserved in the cool of the liquid mud. He tore it open and drank thirstily. Then, dropping the carton – with no need, for once, to look for a bin – he set off cautiously through the trees.

As he trudged on, there were plenty of odd creakings and rustlings to send his heart leaping into his throat, but he saw nothing green and scaly. All that really worried him was that he was no longer sure of the right direction to take. He was disorientated. The easiest way through the trees and the wreckage might not have been the most direct route, but he was too tired and too scared to do anything else.

He had no way of measuring time except for the way the moonlight changed and, at last, faded. By now Jason's feet hurt, and the ache in his leg began to nag him again. He couldn't remember when he had last felt this tired. Unable to go on in the unbroken stillness, he fell down under a tree and slept once more.

Jason woke to the dim light of dawn. His muscles shrieked a protest as he hauled himself up into a sitting position. He shivered: his clothes were wet with dew and daubed with mud. But he was alive, and it was morning.

Jason could see the direction in which the light was strongest. That must be the east. Thankfully, he stumbled off towards it.

Walking grew easier as the stiffness in him wore off. Before long Jason realized that he was approaching the edge of the trees. Through the last, thinning trunks, he could see a road. But when he stepped out on to it, he had no idea which road it was. One side was bounded by trees, the other by a rocky, sandy bluff. There were no signs to point him in one direction or the other.

Rubbing his eyes, he forced his tired mind to work and decided what to do. The brightest part of the sky, where the sun would come up, showed him which way was east. Jason could not imagine that he had circled the town during the night, so he needed to go south – along the road to his right. He turned in that direction and set off.

Moving along the road was easier than struggling through the trees. Here and there, a tree had fallen, and sometimes a landslide from the bluff on the left had spilt sand and stones on to the surface of the road, but mostly it was clear. All the same, trudging along, making an effort to put one foot in front of the other, Jason wished for a car.

From wishing, it did not take long for him to start looking for one. His father had taught him to drive on their own land, even though Jason was still too young to hold a licence. Jason remembered steering the truck down the long, straight avenues of trees at picking time. A car would get him into town faster. Surely no cops, even if they saw him, would pull him in for trying to save his father's life?

His father. Jason's mind wandered back to the grove. Was he already dead? Were his own efforts already all for nothing? He steeled himself against such negative thoughts and concentrated on cars. He had to find a car.

The first vehicle Jason saw was obviously no good. Along a stretch of the road, where a gully ran alongside it, the surface had crumbled, as if the stones beneath it had been washed away. There was a car, nose down in the channel, its back wheels raised off the ground, its windscreen smashed and the shiny red bonnet crumpled. No one was in sight; its driver must have got out safely. Jason left it and tramped on.

By now the sky was blue and the sun was up, its rays warming his face and drying his matted hair. Jason's clothes began to steam gently as the air grew warmer. It was going to be a beautiful, peaceful day.

The next car Jason found was a beauty: a little sports model just like Sally's, but silver-blue. It was parked at the end of a track leading off the road to a house. Jason could see that the track ended abruptly – but there was no sign of a house. If there ever had been one, the whole site had been completely levelled.

Jason was puzzled to think who might have left the car like that, or how it had survived the wind. He was itching to get behind the wheel and drive it away. But when he crossed the road to look at it, there were no keys in it. Jason stood and stared at it. He knew there was a way of starting it without keys, but he didn't know how to do it. He kicked the front tyre with his foot with frustration.

Feeling miserable and disappointed, he left the car and went on. The sick fear about his father was growing inside him again, forcing its way back into his thoughts. This was taking too long. Somebody as badly hurt as his dad *must* have died during the night. He might as well sit down and stop trying – wait for somebody to come by and pick him up.

But he kept walking.

The town was still out of sight, and Jason had almost given up hope of finding a car when he saw it. A real old clunker, its doors scabbed with rust and caked with a decade of dirt. It was slewed sideways across the road and its back wheels were buried in loose soil and stones from a landslide. Jason crept up to it almost as if he was stalking an animal.

His heart was pumping as he peered in through the side window; the keys were still in the ignition. He opened the door, slid behind the wheel and fastened the seat belt. If the car was out of fuel . . .

He twisted the key. The engine turned over but did not fire. Jason clenched his teeth. He felt for the choke, eased it out gently and tried again. This time the engine caught briefly but then died.

Jason sat back, breathing deeply. Much more of this, and he would flatten the battery. One more time. Just a bit more choke. Switch on, tap the accelerator . . .

The engine roared into life.

Jason gripped the steering wheel with elation. He was still lost in the excitement and the welcome sound of the purring engine when he caught a flicker of movement in the rear-view mirror.

He stared and his foot slipped off the pedal. The engine coughed and spluttered into silence. A shapeless mound was heaving itself up from the rear seat and, as Jason tried to turn, a hand gripped his shoulder.

CHAPTER TWELVE

For just a few seconds, all the monsters that Jason had ever seen in the late-night horror movies gibbered and squirmed through his mind. His heart thumping, he twisted around in the driver's seat of the beat-up old car and faced whatever it was behind him.

A man was sitting on the dusty back seat, with a rug draped round his shoulders. One hand grasped Jason, the other hung awkwardly, as if it was injured. It wasn't a monster, but to Jason the man was almost as scary. He had a wild look about him, untidy hair and beard, and red-rimmed eyes. He was wearing a torn plaid shirt.

Jason pulled away from the clutching fingers. 'Quit it!' he snapped. He tried to sound angry, to hide how frightened he'd been.

'What you doing, kid?' the man said. His voice was hoarse. 'You planning on stealing this car?'

'No,' Jason mumbled quickly. 'I was just – just borrowing it. My dad's hurt. I need to get help.'

'You can drive, then, kid?'

Jason nodded.

The man watched him for a minute, pulling the rug round him awkwardly with one hand. Jason stared back, and his gaze fell on the man's limp arm.

'OK, OK,' said the man defensively, as if he'd just been interrogated by the police. 'It's broke. Did it in the hurricane, yesterday, like the fool I am. I can't drive, so you can take us *both* into town.' Then the man flopped back and fell silent. That seemed to be as much as he was going to say.

Jason paused before reaching for the ignition key again. He took a deep breath. His initial fright was ebbing away – he figured he could outrun the man, if it came to that.

'What you waiting for, kid?' the man asked impatiently.

Jason turned the key again; this time the engine sprang to life first time and ticked over smoothly. From the gauge on the dashboard, Jason saw that the petrol tank was about a quarter full – easily enough to get them into town.

First gear. Easy on the accelerator. The back wheels spun on the dirt and stones, but the car refused to move.

'Needs more grip,' the man said flatly from the back seat.

Jason put the engine back in neutral. The car was idling comfortably. He looked wildly around and then glanced down at his feet. The knobbly black rubber floor-mats would be perfect.

Knowing that the man wouldn't be of any help to him, Jason got out of the car and fitted two mats carefully under each of the back wheels. Then he got in and tried again.

First gear, accelerator pedal, the wheels spun – biting on the matting and the road. The car lurched forward.

Jason spun the wheel and slammed a foot down on the brake. The engine coughed and nearly stalled. Frantically Jason pressed the accelerator again and the engine recovered. The car kept moving, but it was going the wrong way. Jason swept the car round in a wide semi-circle, turning the wheel full lock.

The man in the back cursed as the car hit a

rock and bumped over it, jolting his injured arm. Jason ignored him. He needed to concentrate all his attention on driving.

At last he was travelling in the right direction. Gripping the steering wheel with taut, outstretched arms, he dared to change up to second, third and then fourth gear as his confidence grew. He passed a speed limit sign, checked that he wasn't going too fast, and then had to stifle his sudden impulse to burst out laughing.

Jason *wanted* to drive fast. Partly because he was worried about his father, partly because he was just so excited to be behind the wheel and moving. It felt as if he was making progress. It took all his self-control not to stamp the accelerator down to the floor and go roaring down the road. But he knew how stupid that would be. The surface wasn't clear; branches were strewn across it and there was mud where the bank at the side of the road had given way.

There was no other traffic – nothing for him to hit – and no one in sight who might stop him and ask questions. He kept going, slowly and carefully.

'You don't drive too bad, kid,' the man said after a while, sounding more friendly. 'What's your name?'

'Jason Mitchell.'

'Pleased to meet you, Jason Mitchell. I'm Dave.'

Jason wondered whether the man was telling the truth. How had he really broken his arm? He'd not been driving. The car was untouched so he couldn't have been in an accident with it. Jason guessed that he had taken shelter in it the night before, to sleep. It would have been poor protection from the hurricane itself. So where had the man been?

The road began to wind downhill, and Jason's mind returned to his driving. At last he felt as if he might be getting somewhere. There were advertising hoardings along the verges – or at least there *had* been hoardings. Most of them were smashed now, just making more obstacles on the road. Added to Jason's worries was the thought of a puncture from nails or splintered wood.

They began to pass houses, all of them showing some signs of storm damage. They were widely spaced, their entrances blocked by closed gates. He could see no sign of life, and he didn't think it was worth stopping to see if he could find a working telephone. Besides, he wasn't sure what his passenger would do if he tried to stop.

The effort of driving was beginning to tire

him. His back ached and his injured leg was growing stiff and painful. He remembered how both his mum and dad used to sit in the driver's seat, relaxed, driving for hours if they had to. Maybe there was more to it than Jason had thought.

The houses became more frequent, until they were lining both sides of the road, which widened out into a dual carriageway with ornamental shrubs planted down the middle. Everything was torn or flattened in the wake of the storm. But at last Jason recognized where he was. He was in one of the new residential estates on the edge of town. He was not far from school, and not far from his Uncle Paul's house.

Now Jason had to decide whether to keep the car or not. It would certainly get him where he needed to go faster, and Dave might turn nasty if Jason didn't do as he was told; but if anyone saw him, he might find himself in trouble, and explanations would slow him down.

He also had to decide where to go. The obvious place was the hospital, but that was on the opposite side of town. There would be a disaster centre, to help survivors and to get essential repairs started as soon as possible, but he didn't know where that was. They'd lost touch with the world before any of that kind of information had filtered through.

Jason sighed deeply as he saw the first signs of life.

A dog ran across the road and dashed between two houses.

Then he saw a man walking along the footpath on his left carrying a long plank of wood. A hundred metres further on, he saw two people pulling window shutters away from a house that was set back from the road. The sight and sound of people working, clearing up and attempting to get their lives back to normal soon became commonplace.

One or two people looked up from their labours as they drove past, and Jason suspected they were giving him funny looks. His ears itched as he listened for a police siren.

What he heard instead, just ahead and to his right, was the noise of confused crashing and shouting, and the piercing sound of breaking glass. The car was passing a side road with a row of shops beyond it, and he saw a whole bunch of people, running and struggling. Automatically he pressed the accelerator to speed up and stay away from trouble. Just then, something struck the car and the windscreen shattered into a thousand stars.

Dave yelled something. Jason panicked and

slammed on the brake, wrenching the wheel around; he could see nothing through the milky, crazed surface in front of him. The car slowed and then jolted to a standstill. Jason was jerked forward, but his seat belt held him. Dave thumped into the seat behind him, and he heard the front bumper crunch sickeningly against something he could not see.

Sheer fury exploded inside him. Jason flung open the door and lurched outside to find out who was throwing stuff at *his* car and threatening *his* life.

'What do you think you're doing, you stupid –!'

He stopped yelling; no one was taking any notice of him. A fracas was surging along the front of the shops. More glass broke. Jason began to understand what was going on, remembering the supermarket where he and Tom had tried to buy supplies.

These guys were looters.

One of the stores sold hi-fi equipment; several figures had broken into it and were helping themselves, looting the goods and fighting over them. Some of the people were waving bottles around. Maybe they'd looted a liquor store first. Most of them were young, not much older than Jason himself. The scene looked ugly. If the cops arrived, he might find himself pulled in together with them, and not just for borrowing a car.

Jason decided that it wouldn't be a good idea to be found anywhere near the car, which was now nuzzling close up to a street light, its bumper buckled and a headlamp smashed. Dave had opened the rear door and was peering out, looking dazed.

'I'm out of here,' Jason said to himself.

He was about to turn and run when he caught sight of someone else in the middle of the fight: a smaller figure, with long, white-blonde hair. A girl who should definitely not have been anywhere near there. The boys were pushing her back and forth from one to another, and she was yelling fit to burst; but to Jason it sounded more like fury than fear. At the same instant he realized that he knew her: Lindy Johnson, the daughter of his school principal.

Generally, Lindy scared him. She was a real hot-shot, so far ahead of him in brains and looks that she was out of sight. Jason could not have imagined Lindy in any sort of trouble she couldn't control – but he was seeing it now. His mind said, 'Don't mess with these guys. Think about Dad!' At the same time his feet, not listening to common sense, were hurling him across the road towards the fight.

'Lindy!' he shouted. 'Get out of there!'

Regardless of whether she was ignoring him or simply had not heard him, Lindy carried on yelling at the other guys. 'Listen! There's people dying down there! I need help!' she pleaded.

Jason cannoned into someone holding a bottle. It flew from the boy's grasp and smashed on the ground. Almost instantly the reek of whisky filled the air. Someone else grabbed Jason by the back of the neck in a powerful grip. He twisted around, trying to glimpse his attacker, but all he could see was a huge shape looming over him. He kicked out backwards, and felt his heel strike a shin bone.

'Hey! Let go!' he panted, feeling the force on his neck lessen a little.

Lindy had managed to pull herself free of the guy who was holding her, but she didn't try to run. She just stood there, fists clenched, yelling. Her hair was tangled, her face scarlet and smeared with mud, and her shirt torn. She looked just as battered as Jason felt. She glanced across and stared into his eyes.

Then she suddenly stopped yelling, but her mouth remained open.

'Jason Mitchell!' she said incredulously.

'Hi,' said Jason feebly.

He drove an elbow into the chest of the guy

who still held him by the neck like a wet cat. It felt like hitting rock.

'I said, let go!' he screamed again.

He still wasn't sure if these guys were just horsing around or if they were going to get really nasty. They stank of alcohol, possessed incredible strength and didn't seem to care what they did or who saw them. Lindy wasn't going to get the help she needed round here. Jason didn't want to hang around to find out how far they were all willing to go in pursuit of teenage kicks.

A figure stepped up to him and drove a fist into his stomach. 'You lookin' for trouble, eh? Well, you've got it!' he grumbled.

Jason doubled over, fighting for breath. Through a red haze he saw Lindy stamp on his attacker's foot. The guy spun around and made a grab for her arm.

Jason's anger boiled over again. He'd survived a hurricane, had his house ripped apart, his dad lay dying in the middle of untold devastation, his first car was wrapped round a lamp-post, and now a bunch of mindless creeps was trying to hold him up! He charged, head down, at the nearest looter. He caught a glimpse of Lindy clinging to the back of another of them, tugging his long, greasy hair.

For a while they were winning, but it

couldn't last. Jason knew it couldn't. They were badly outnumbered. This mob was too big and mean, and they were only temporarily confused by the temerity he and Lindy showed by fighting back. The gang would soon overpower them when they pulled themselves together.

We're going to be hamburger, Jason thought.

CHAPTER THIRTEEN

The sound that Jason had feared hearing for so long suddenly became music to his ears. The distinctive siren of a police patrol car cut across the confrontation and caused an immediate hush.

The guy who was trying to bounce Jason on the pavement let go, and seconds later all the looters were scattering across the paths. They piled into an old station wagon and skidded on to the road in a cloud of exhaust fumes, just as the cop car appeared round the corner and immediately wailed off in pursuit.

At the same moment, Jason looked up to see Dave, cradling his broken arm, go shambling across the road and disappear down a side street. He hadn't wanted to meet the authorities either.

It figured.

Jason and Lindy were left looking at each other in front of the wrecked shop, with glass and bits of electrical equipment strewn all round them. Jason gasped for lungfuls of air, trying to decide which part of him ached worst. 'What was all that about?' he asked, breathlessly.

Lindy tucked strands of hair behind her ears. 'Sorry,' she replied, biting her lip. 'I guess I lost it. I was looking for help, but those goons wouldn't listen.' Lindy looked him up and down briefly. 'I guess you're better than nothing. Come on!'

She set off down the road with a determined stride.

Looking back over her shoulder, she shouted, 'Hurry up!'

'I can't!' Jason spluttered. 'My Dad –'

But Lindy wasn't listening. He watched the back of her head for a moment, willing her to turn around and see the expression on his face. But she didn't. Jason sighed deeply. At least she was moving in the right direction – towards the centre of town. If he went with her, he might find the help he was looking for himself.

He broke into a run and caught her up. 'Where've you been? How you did you survive it? Where're we going?' he asked, scanning the damaged houses all around and the litter clogging the footpaths. 'I thought our place looked bad but this . . . this is virtually a total wipeout.'

Lindy didn't look at him. 'The movie theatre collapsed,' she said. Her voice was angry. 'Dad sent me to get help. There's people trapped in there.'

'The movie theatre? You went to the movies in the middle of a hurricane?'

Lindy shot him a withering look. 'Jason Mitchell, you haven't the faintest idea what's been happening in this town, have you?' She was heading downhill towards the town centre, almost running, but still with enough breath to talk. 'Mom and Dad volunteered to stay and help at the disaster centre,' she explained. 'Mom's a nurse, you know? And they let me and Nick – you know Nick, my brother? – they let us stay with them. The rescue services took over some civil offices near the hospital. Yesterday, when school was out, we went down there and started getting ready for casualties.'

'Did the hurricane flatten everything?' Jason could just about keep up with her. Apart from Dave, he hadn't spoken to anyone for twelve hours. He was desperate to fill in the gaps in his own knowledge of the storm with the details of how it had hit town.

'It was like nothing I've ever seen before,

Jason. Like nothing *anybody* has ever seen. We were in the basement at the town hall and did OK. Afterwards, we were told that some of the streets were flooded. Along the beach was the worst. Everything was smashed up. Some of the submerged houses had people sitting on the roofs, you know. Like you see on the news.'

Her voice shook as she spoke the last few words, and she set her mouth determinedly.

'And you know what was really spooky, Jason?' she went on. 'There were cars under the water, and some of them had their lights on, and their horns were sounding, just as if their drivers were still sitting in them. But there wasn't anyone. Dad said there must have been a short in their electrics. It was *so* weird.'

Jason tried to imagine the swirling water and the dark sky, the lashing wind and rain, people stranded and shouting for help.

'Loads of people were put in the movie theatre. They had nowhere else to go,' Lindy said, blinking away the tears she had so far managed to hold off. 'The roof fell in, Jason. All those people were buried.' She clenched her fists.

'But the storm was over by then,' Jason said, shocked by the news of this latest tragedy.

'The building was weakened, I guess. Dad sent Nick back to the hospital for help and told me to look for people to shift the wreckage. I found some, and then I ran into those geeks. Thanks for stopping, Jason.'

Jason was surprised to be thanked. He hadn't done much, anyway. He was even more surprised when Lindy smiled at him before saying, 'And you? What are you doing here? I thought you lived out of town.'

'I do. We stayed home, yesterday. The storm blew our house away. My dad's trapped under our car, but he's still alive. At least, he was yesterday when I left.'

Lindy came to a halt and really looked at him for the first time. 'That's tough,' she said. 'I'm really sorry, Jason. Look, come and talk to Dad, OK? He'll know what to do.'

She set off again. Jason followed, some of the weight of worry lifting from him. At least he was getting closer to finding help.

As they drew nearer to the town centre, Jason began to understand what Lindy had been telling him. He could see more of the devastation Hurricane Gordon had left behind.

On one street corner, a couple of dogs were snuffling about in the rubbish. They watched Jason and Lindy pass with bright, hungry eyes. Jason wondered how long it would be, how hungry they would have to be, before they did more than just watch.

As they went on, Jason became used to

skirting round the piles of debris in the road, and when he almost tripped over something sticking out from one of them it took him a few seconds before he realized what it was.

A man's arm. He was lying on his back, and most of his body was covered by a piece of broken board.

'Hey!' Jason called out to Lindy, who was a few paces ahead.

He bent down instinctively, gripped the edge of the board and heaved. The board swung up and back, and Jason looked down at what he had uncovered.

He was a small man, his brown hair streaked with grey. His face was purple. He needed a shave. His eyes were open, staring. At Jason's shoulder, Lindy said, 'He's dead.'

Jason couldn't speak. Did his father look like that by now? Small and broken, tossed aside like a piece of rubbish? Jason felt sweat break out over his body, and he started to shiver. He wanted to be sick.

Lindy tugged at his arm. 'Come on, Jason,' she said sadly. 'We can't do anything here.'

For a second, stupidly, Jason resisted, and then he gave in and let Lindy pull him away, down the road towards the people who could still be helped.

★

In the town centre the streets were too badly blocked to let cars through. Sometimes, even though they were on foot, Jason and Lindy had to climb over obstacles. Jason had thought he was tired before, but now his whole body was one long nagging ache, and he could happily have lain down in the mud and gone to sleep. Only the thought of his dad kept him going.

When they turned the corner of the street where the movie theatre was, Jason sensed at once that something was different. At first he couldn't work out what it was, then he realized that the steeple of the episcopalian church that had always closed off the view at the far end of the street was gone. Instead, he saw the open sky.

Halfway up the street was the collapsed movie theatre. The whole building had folded up like a concertina, spraying bricks and woodwork down the steps and across the pavement. Jason found it hard to imagine that anyone could still be alive under all that.

Several people were picking their way over the mound of debris; some of them had made a human chain and were passing wreckage along it, out of the way.

Near the top of the mound was a man Jason had to look at twice before he recognized him as Mr Johnson. Filthy, with a shadow of stubble and wearing jogging trousers and a sweatshirt, he looked completely unlike their neat, formally dressed Principal.

'Hey, Dad!' Lindy called out, and she went over to talk to him.

Jason stayed where he was, surveying the scene of devastation. A minute later, somebody shoved a section of roof beam into his hands. He found himself part of a human chain, and he passed the beam along to the next person in line.

The helpers seemed to be trying to uncover a section near the centre of the collapsed building. Jason didn't know why, whether they had heard sounds that told them someone was still alive, or whether they just had to start somewhere.

He went on heaving wreckage. Pretty soon he felt there was a rhythm to it. Grab, turn and pass . . . grab, turn and pass, until his back felt like breaking, his hands were torn and grit stung his eyes. And all the while he wondered how this was helping his dad.

While he watched Lindy, animated in her conversation with her father, Mr Johnson was still crouching at the edge of the cleared section. He looked as if he was telling the helpers which piece of debris to move next. Then Jason heard him shout. He bent down into the hole and when he came up again he was holding a small child.

The body hung limp in Mr Johnson's arms.

The chain slowed to a halt as everyone stared. Jason tasted grit on his tongue, remembering the dead man he had found up the street. Then one of the thin legs jerked and there was the sound of feeble crying. At the same moment, another figure, a man this time, crawled out of the hole in the ruins and knelt, blinking in the sunlight. The chain of helpers set up a ragged cheer. Jason couldn't help but join in.

After that, everything seemed to speed up. More people were coming out of the hole, being pulled or lifted out, or making it under their own steam. The chain broke up. At the same time, a couple of paramedics came scrambling along the street, carrying stretchers between them. Jason heard one of them speaking to Mr Johnson.

'We've an ambulance on the corner of Fourth and Park. Can't get no further. Anyone needs treatment and can walk should get along down there.'

'Sure,' the Principal replied, wiping his brow with his dirty sleeve.

Mr Johnson started relaying orders. One or two of the victims got to their feet and stumbled off in the direction he indicated.

Jason edged closer. 'Mr Johnson, sir –' he began desperately.

'Oh, hi, Jason. Lindy told me about you. Take

a ride back to the centre in the ambulance. You'll find somebody there who can help.' The Principal turned to the paramedic, who was strapping someone on to a stretcher, and said, 'Did that helicopter show?'

The paramedic looked up. 'Yeah. Pilot's been in and out all morning.'

'Helicopter?' Jason said, with a sudden stab of hope.

Mr Johnson coughed, and then he grinned. At that moment Jason thought that he looked just like a regular person – not like a school principal at all.

'An army helicopter, to ferry in survivors from out of town,' he explained. 'Sounds just what you need, Jason. Lindy, go with him and show him who to talk to.'

Lindy was hugging a small girl who was wailing loudly for her mother. The child had a cut on her forehead and blood was smeared all over her face. Lindy was smiling and crying at the same time. 'Sure, Dad,' she said.

A few minutes later, Jason found himself carrying one end of a stretcher, manoeuvring it along the street to where the ambulance was parked. Lindy walked beside him, still carrying the little girl, who had now given up crying and had gone to sleep, her head on Lindy's shoulder, her thumb locked in her mouth.

When the ambulance had taken on as many victims as it could carry, and Jason had clambered aboard, it started off, siren blaring. It moved fast; after a few minutes he stopped looking out of the open rear doors, which wouldn't close, and he stopped flinching every time the vehicle hurtled round another heap of wreckage.

The hospital looked as if it had escaped the worst of the storm damage. Other ambulances were arriving too – passing them at speed and then leaving again. As their ambulance drew to a halt, Lindy grabbed Jason and dragged him out. 'This way,' she said urgently.

She led him, half pushing, half dragging, along a path through the hospital grounds. Her energy and drive were still undiminished – if anything, they were enhanced by the successful outcome at the collapsed movie theatre.

The surrounding gardens were landscaped with grass and trees and usually were quiet and peaceful. Now they looked like an army camp. Jason gaped at the tents, and at soldiers hurrying back and forth. He wondered if someone had declared war while he wasn't looking.

He and Lindy passed a group of soldiers working at a field kitchen, with people standing in line waiting for food. Jason remembered how hungry he was, but there was no time for him to wait. He just cast a longing glance over one shoulder, and followed Lindy.

A moment later, she cried out, 'Look!'

Jason followed her finger, pointing high into the sky. He saw a small helicopter rapidly growing larger. Seconds later, he heard the sound of its engine. Lindy quickened her pace to a run, and Jason managed to squeeze out just enough energy to do the same.

The helicopter roared above them – replicating the thunderous noise Jason had first heard the previous day when he had been sheltering inside his old home, buffeted by the winds. The metal bird landed on a flat stretch of ground behind the hospital buildings. As Lindy and Jason approached, they saw a couple of paramedics start to manoeuvre a stretcher with someone strapped to it down to the ground.

Dad could be next, Jason thought.

As the paramedics went past with the stretcher, Lindy pushed Jason towards the pilot. 'Go on, tell him!' she screamed above the rotating helicopter blades, which were slowing down – but were still deafening.

The pilot had pulled off his helmet, and he jumped down to the ground as well. He leant against the clear windows of the helicopter cockpit. He was a tall, youngish man with short, jet-black hair, and he looked tired.

Jason went up to him. 'Uh . . . sir?' Jason asked tentatively.

'Yeah?'

Jason felt like an idiot, even though his need was so urgent. He wondered whether the pilot would listen to a kid like him, when there must be hundreds of other people needing help – all of them just as desperate as him. If not more so.

But he explained what had happened, nevertheless. It all came out in a torrent of tangled description and warped chronology. His dad was trapped underneath some cars, he was probably already dead, his house was gone, his mum was OK, he'd been on the road since last night.

He hadn't finished speaking when the pilot suddenly hauled himself back into the cockpit, snapped a few words into his radio, and listened to the reply.

Jason still had his mouth open in mid-sentence when the pilot pushed his helmet back on to his head and flipped down the lenses of his reflective goggles.

Then he leant down towards Jason and grinned.

'OK, kid. You got yourself a helicopter.'

CHAPTER FOURTEEN

Jason sat in the helicopter cockpit – his stomach a tangled knot of tension. Now that he had found help, he was suddenly aware of every second that was running away, slipping by and lengthening the odds that he would find his father still alive. Safely fastened to his seat, he clenched his fists anxiously.

Behind him, two paramedics, carrying an empty stretcher, leapt into the draughty hold and slammed the door shut behind them. The helicopter pilot nodded at him and began preparing for flight. A rhythmic hum erupted above his head and the volume of noise from the rotating blades steadily increased.

Lindy Johnson stepped back from the craft and smiled at him. She started to wave. Jason looked at her and waved back. He so was grateful for everything that the Principal's daughter had done for him in the past few hours. As Jason's stomach lurched and the ground fell away beneath him, he realized too late that he hadn't really thanked her properly. She soon became a tiny figure on the green patchwork garden behind the hospital buildings.

When it was all over, when life had returned to normal, and he was back at school – then he'd find her again and talk to her. Really talk to her. They shared something now. It was a terrible thing to have in common, though. Two young people brought together in the aftermath of Hurricane Gordon – Lindy's worst nightmare memories would be etched on her brain for ever. Looking down over swarming figures below, Jason couldn't help but think his worst terror was still to come.

The sun's rays cut through the thin clouds and cast a shadow from the helicopter on to the devastated town below. For a while Jason watched their shadow bobbing over the wrecked buildings and flattened houses.

To the south, the streets were choked with rubble. In the town centre, cars littered the streets at awkward angles – some were even upside down. Worse still, as the helicopter banked to Jason's right and sped up the coast, whole streets looked as if they had been splintered into firewood. Huge pools of water reflected light back up at him.

Jason clung to the inside of the helicopter, his ears filled with the whirr of the rotor blades and an occasional crackle from the radio. Craning around, he watched the two paramedics, who were also looking out through a thin, open hatchway, while the gusting wind blew their hair round their faces. One was a man, solid and grey-haired, and the other a woman, younger, slim and alert. They gave off an ultra-professional appearance in their light-green jumpsuits, and Jason sure hoped they knew their job.

Jason could see the line of the beach and the sea washing in, edged by a white froth of foam. At first he wasn't quite sure what he was looking at. Then, as he worked out how things should be on the ground, he realized that a whole line of beach cabins – a regular holiday village – had completely disappeared. A little further north, there had been a pretty harbour where sailing boats were moored; now the sea had gouged out an even deeper bay, and there was no sign of boats or buildings. The whole shape of the coast had changed.

While Jason was looking down, the helicopter banked inland, and Jason overheard the pilot muttering indistinctly into his radio – giving and receiving instructions.

The pilot spat out his mouthpiece and looked briefly across at him. 'North of town, yeah? The Mitchell place? Can you give me a landmark?'

Jason nodded and peered down again. Now they were flying over the strip of citrus groves that ran all along this part of the coast. Jason had never thought about how his own home would look from the air. 'There's a dirt road off the freeway . . .' he began.

Jason realized, as he spoke, that the pilot might not be able to see the road any longer: too many trees had been blown across it. He himself didn't recognize anything below him. The landscape was brown instead of green; the leaves had been stripped from the trees. The helicopter flew over one area where each tree had been neatly felled, and the trunks lay, side by side, like a row of pencils.

'I don't know . . .' Jason said desperately. He didn't want to fail now.

'Don't worry, kid,' the pilot said reassuringly. 'We'll find it. Keep looking, and yell if you see some place you know.'

Jason kept looking, his eyes fixed on the

devastated trees below. The helicopter was following the line of the freeway, and already cars were returning; people racing south, Jason guessed, to find out what was left of their homes.

Then he saw something that brought him upright in his seat: a thin column of smoke rising from the trees ahead. 'There!' he pointed, waving his arm in front of him.

He couldn't know that he was right, not yet; but a wash of relief enveloped him. His mum had said she would make some kind of signal for the rescue services. A moment later, he knew for certain that he was right as the helicopter flew over a clearing and Jason looked down on the wreck of his house and the garage where his father was trapped.

'We found it!' he cried.

The pilot circled once, establishing the terrain below. Then he expertly set the helicopter down in the clearing in front of the house at the end of the partially covered dirt road. Jason returned to earth with only the slightest bump.

He jumped out of the cockpit and looked around frantically. He couldn't see any sign of life, only a bonfire in front of the garage doorway, burning sluggishly and sending up its thread of smoke.

'Mom!' he called out. 'Mom!'

He ran across to the garage but, before he could reach it, Abby Mitchell appeared in the doorway, rubbing a hand over her eyes.

'Jason,' she gasped. 'You're home. Sorry, I guess I fell asleep in there.'

Jason rushed forward and hugged her. He quickly let go, stood back and looked into her eyes. 'Dad. Is he . . .?'

Abby rubbed her hand over her eyes again. 'He's OK, Jason. Well, no, not OK, but he's alive.' She gave Jason the ghost of a grin. 'Too stubborn to give up, your father.' She looked across at the helicopter behind him and at the figures dismounting. 'You've been busy.'

The paramedics came to join them and Abby shook their hands, welcoming them as if she still had a house and they were dropping by for coffee.

'He's in here?' the man said, looking serious. 'Let's take a look.'

Abby led the way into the garage, edging round the piled machinery.

Jason followed them in. He glanced around and thought that nothing much had changed since the day before. His father was still lying inside the cave made by the piled-up cars. Abby had put a rolled-up blanket under his head and had wrapped him in Great-

Grandma's patchwork quilt. Jason couldn't help grinning when he saw that.

As he looked down at his father, Drake Mitchell's eyes fluttered open. He gazed at Jason in an unfocused sort of way and said very faintly, 'Hi, son.'

Jason felt his grin growing wider, and at the same time, stupidly, he wanted to burst into tears.

'Right,' the female paramedic said, taking over. 'We need to get these cars off him. We need space.'

The man knelt down and wedged one shoulder under the roof of the upside-down station wagon. His companion took up position a bit further along.

'Watch the small car,' the pilot said across them all. He was standing, looking on, in the doorway. 'Unless you get lucky, that could come down on top of him.'

Abby and the pilot moved forward and took hold of the smaller car's bumper.

'Right,' the pilot said, taking control. 'When I say heave – heave.'

Everyone braced themselves against whatever part of the unstable structure they were holding.

'One, two, three . . . heave!'

There was a grinding sound, followed by a

clattering as small pieces of metal sprang away. Gradually, ponderously, the station wagon was lifted out of the main heap. As it rose, Jason instinctively dived underneath and helped to push. At the same moment the small car shifted; Abby and the pilot yanked, and it bounced down on the garage floor right next to where Drake Mitchell was lying.

For a dizzying second Jason thought that the station wagon was going to fall back and crush them all. Then it tilted and slid and crashed to the garage floor. Loose metal rattled and pattered into silence.

Jason let out a long breath and rubbed his hands over his face. Already the two paramedics were clearing the remaining wreckage that still lay across his father's legs. Together with the pilot, they carefully lifted the limp body on to the stretcher and strapped him in.

'He'll be fine,' the woman said, as they bundled him out of the garage and into the bright light.

Jason and his mother exchanged relieved looks.

They followed the helicopter crew back to the giant metal bird and watched as they began to load Drake on to his stretcher, just as Jason had imagined back at the hospital.

'Are you coming with us?' the pilot asked. 'There's shelters in town where you could stay.'

'Well, I guess –' Abby began.

'No.' A weak voice interrupted her. Drake Mitchell, lying on his stretcher, raised his head a fraction. 'Stay here. Mustn't leave the property . . .'

Abby and Jason looked at each other. Abby sighed.

Jason felt himself starting to grin.

'No, Drake. I'm coming with you. You do as you're told for once.' Abby's voice was sharp. Then she bent down towards her husband, putting her hand over his. 'We *will* live here again,' she said. 'But there's a lot to be done before then.'

Drake didn't reply but, as the paramedics strapped him firmly into place in the helicopter, his eyes were on his son; Jason thought that he could see a look of approval on his father's face.

'Heaven help the nurse who has to look after him,' Abby said.

Jason watched the activity going on round him and felt a tremendous sense of achievement. He had made it back in time and his dad wasn't going to die. Tom would be back as soon as he found a way through. And

Jason couldn't wait to see Bethy again – even if she was a real pain sometimes.

When his father's stretcher was in position, Jason climbed up into the helicopter. Abby followed him.

'Well, here we go,' she said, steeling herself for the forthcoming rollercoaster ride in the sky. She paused, then added, 'You did well, Jason. Really well.'

Embarrassed, Jason was trying to think of something to reply when his mother suddenly grabbed his arm.

'Jason, will you look over there!' she said in a strange voice.

Jason looked. Tiger the cat had just come into sight round the corner of the machine store, fastidiously picking up each paw and shaking it as if he hated the wet grass.

'Tiger!' Jason called. 'Where did he come from?'

'I don't know,' Abby said. 'But he survived.'

'Well, sure.' Jason felt laughter bubbling up inside him. 'He's a Mitchell cat.'

The pilot was about to start the helicopter's engine.

'Hey, wait!' Jason cried, leaning forward into the cockpit.

He scrambled down from the helicopter again, swooped on Tiger and picked him up in his arms, hugging him. Tiger writhed furiously and swatted him. Jason dropped the cat and sucked his scratched wrist.

'Is that all the thanks I get?' he said, frowning.

Jason grabbed Great-Grandma's patchwork quilt, which was lying, discarded, on the ground, dropped it over Tiger and bundled him up. Only Tiger's head poked out, yowling.

Abby was leaning down from the helicopter. Jason handed the parcel of Tiger up to her, then hauled himself up into the craft.

'You folks quite ready?' the pilot said, grinning.

The engine whine rose and the helicopter took off. Jason felt the familiar lurching as it lifted above the trees. While Abby held Tiger on her lap, he stared down at his ruined home. At first it filled his vision but, as the helicopter gained height and headed south, the wreckage grew smaller and even the signal smoke disappeared. He turned away and looked at his mother.

'OK,' he said. 'What do we do next?'

HURRICANES

THE ESSENTIAL SURVIVAL GUIDE

Hurricanes are the strongest storm
winds in the world.
They are spectacular on a massive
scale, unstoppable and terrifying.

If a hurricane hits you with its full might,
this is what you can expect:

●

Swirling winds that hit you with the
force of a brick wall

●

Flattened houses, overturned cars,
upturned trees and millions of pounds
of damage

●

All your treasured possessions wiped
away in seconds

●

Torrential rain that knocks you off your
feet

●

Colossal tidal waves and flash floods
that can wreck entire coastal areas

●

No escape from a deafening
wall of noise

HURRICANES KILL

Warnings

If a hurricane is heading towards your area,
warnings will be issued by the police and local
authorities:
a) in newspapers
b) via radio
c) on TV

Keep Listening!
Your portable radio is essential – don't lose it.

You will be told:
a) Where the hurricane is expected to strike.
b) The severity and likely scale of the storm.
c) When to evacuate your home.
d) The safest areas to go to.
e) The best routes to take.

Keep Listening!
The information may change. Your life could
depend on it.

DO travel by the route you have been given.
DON'T try to find a better way. Experts have
designed your escape to keep traffic jams to a
minimum.
DO avoid troublemakers. Some people take
advantage of disaster situations and stay behind
to loot shops and homes.
DON'T try to be a hero if someone causes
trouble. The authorities will take care of
lawbreakers.

3

Be Prepared!

Stay calm. Panic and silly arguments can break out when you are under pressure to do something quickly. Keep cool and don't lose your head.

Take Charge. Decide who is going to organize your evacuation and agree a checklist of things to do – and who is going to do them.

Your Pets
● As soon as the hurricane warning is given, secure all your pets indoors.

● Prepare their carriers or travelling cages for the journey and think about what they will need.

● Don't spend valuable time looking for your pet when the time to leave comes close. There is nothing you can do. You must trust the animal's good sense – natural instinct will usually tell them where to shelter.

Your Home
Your home is at risk during severe hurricanes, but you can take precautions to minimize the impending damage.

● Clear away any loose and unsecured items you may have outdoors. This includes dustbins, garden chairs, tables or signs – anything that

might be blown or washed away. Store them
inside your house or garage.

Danger!
Flying objects can cause serious injuries

● All windows should be boarded up with strong
wooden planks. Glass is easily smashed by flying
wreckage. Use mattresses and other furniture to
help secure windows and doors. If you already
have shutters, check these are properly closed
before you leave.

● In case of flooding, move as much of your furniture as you can to the upper part of the house
or into a loft or attic if your home is single-storey.

● Hide smaller items and your more valuable
things in cupboards and secure containers like
trunks, tea-chests or in strong cardboard boxes.
Unsecured homes are an open invitation to
thieves.

● Wrap blankets around precious and breakable
objects to protect against buffeting and water-
damage.

● Unplug electrical equipment – including
fridges, freezers and TVs. Do not touch any items
which may already be wet.

Danger!
Electric shocks can kill

● Turn off supplies of gas, electricity and water.

● Store clean drinking water in jugs, baths or cans and other containers indoors – just in case you are cut off at the last minute.

● Close all internal doors before you leave.

● Make sure drains, drainpipes and guttering are clear of dirt and blockages in order to cope with the massive amounts of rainwater expected.

● Don't use sandbags around your basement or cellar to keep water out. Seepage can penetrate the earth around the building, collect and cause huge structural damage.

● Lock doors and windows to deter housebreakers.

Your Car
Make sure your escape vehicle is ready for the long journey ahead.

● Check you have enough petrol. It will soon become unavailable as petrol stations and garages close. Fill up when you hear the first warning.

● Take an extra can of fuel in the boot or trunk of your vehicle – just in case.

● Check that all tyre pressures, oil and water levels are as they should be.

● Go to the bathroom before you leave. Your journey will be long and may be scary. Stopping for regular toilet breaks could be catastrophic.

● Don't overfill suitcases or your vehicle. This can make your car unwieldy, difficult to drive and may cause injury if you have to brake or stop suddenly for a hazard on your journey.

● Take your most essential possessions and smaller things of value. Keep vital documents, money, bank cards and some forms of identification with you at all times.

● Make sure you have enough food and water to last the entire length of your journey. Don't assume that any shops along your route will be open. Tradespeople must evacuate too.

Evacuate!

On the Move!
● Swallow or press your ears to make them 'pop' to relieve the pressure.

● Decide who is going to sit where in the car. You know who'll get on and who won't. If you can't stand sitting next to your brother, sister or someone else on the ride, don't even try.

● Don't make a pressure-keg situation worse by arguing. The battering winds and long, slow progress will make you stressed enough as it is.

● Don't distract your driver. Negotiating the evacuation route will take total concentration.

● Look out for any potential hazards on the road and give the driver advance warnings.

Danger!
Heavy rain, fallen trees or fallen cables can make driving dangerous

Stranded
If you are marooned in your vehicle:
a) Turn off the engine. Avoid producing dangerous fumes and wasting petrol.
b) Keep warm.
c) Eat and drink regularly.
d) Be careful when opening your vehicle doors. Hold on tight. Slamming doors caused by strong winds can cause injury.

Hurricane Strike!

If the worst happens and you are caught out in the open when the full force of a hurricane strikes, you can take some precautions to increase your likelihood of survival:

● Look for shelter immediately. Massive concrete or brick structures, such as bridges, underpasses or even the bases of high-rise buildings can give shelter from the worst winds.

● Avoid sheltering near drains, rivers or other places where water collects.

Danger!
Storm waters can rise almost instantly and sweep you away in a flash flood

● In wide-open spaces, seek shelter away from clumps of trees – branches and entire trees will be blown down and could crush you.

● Protect your head. Use a T-shirt to cover your eyes. The driving rain will sting.

● From time to time move your legs, arms and your whole body to avoid chills and cramps.

● Try to avoid sleeping. Concentrate on staying alive.

● Stay as close to the ground as possible and tuck your knees under your body.

● If you try to stand, you will be blown away.

9

Hurricanes
- The Facts

Where?
Hurricanes only develop at sea and only over warm water – mainly in tropical regions bordering the Equator.

When?
January is the peak time for hurricanes in the southern hemisphere, September and October for the western Atlantic and Pacific oceans. Between June and October they bombard the western coast of the USA and the Caribbean.

How?
Hurricances begin as a small amount of warm air rising. As the air climbs it meets colder air and heat is released as energy. The turning earth begins to spin the warm air outwards, faster and faster, until the resulting winds reach hurricane strength.

Effect?
Hurricanes are natural phenomena that have existed for thousands of years and that have helped shape parts of the earth's face.
They can cause immense destruction, sweeping away anything in their path. Hurricanes often take many lives and can cripple the economies of whole countries.

10

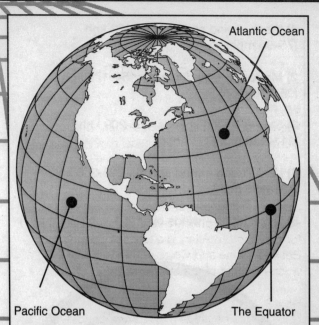

Atlantic Ocean

Pacific Ocean

The Equator

Size does matter!

For a tropical storm to become a hurricane, its
wind speed must reach more than 120 kph
(75 mph). The average hurricane is nearly circular
in shape and 800 km (500 miles) in diameter. It
lasts for about 10 days and covers huge distances.
Areas as big as the West Indies could be entirely
covered and attacked at the same time by one
enormous storm system.

There are five different strengths, each giving a
rough idea of the power of the expected hurricane:

1) Weak – wind speeds 120–153 kph (75–95 mph)

2) Moderate – wind speeds 154–177 kph (96–110 mph)

3) Strong – wind speeds 178–209 kph (111–130 mph)

4) Very Strong – wind speeds 210–250 kph (131–155 mph)

5) Devastating – winds over 251 kph (156 mph+)

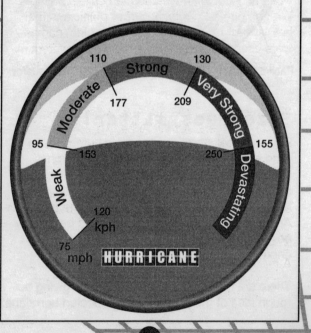

What's in a name?

The word hurricane comes from 'huricon' – the West Indian word for 'big wind'. In the Pacific, hurricanes are known as typhoons, as taino in Haiti and as baguio in the Philippines. In the Far East they are called cyclones, and in Australia willy-willies!

Every hurricane is given a male or a female name. Each year, the first hurricane will be given a name starting with the letter A, the second the letter B, and so on. The system began in 1890 when an Australian weatherman called Clement Wragge named hurricanes after politicians that he disliked! After several protests, girls' names were used instead. Then, in 1979, the system changed again and every second hurricane now has a male name.

'A' names have included: Ana, Andrew, Alice, Anthony, Angela, Arthur, Anne, Alan, Alysha, Amos, Audrey, Adolph, Ava, Adrian, Arlene, Andrez, Alicia.

'B' names have included: Betty, Babe, Bernice, Brett, Beatrice, Bill, Bianca, Barry, Barbara.

Power

A moderately sized hurricane gusting at more than 154 kph (96 mph) produces more energy than a nuclear explosion.

Waterworlds

Hurricanes cause sea water in the affected area to rise above the normal high-tide mark. The sea water is driven by the down force of the hurricane wind towards the shore. This storm surge can be huge. In a weak hurricane, sea levels can be 1.5 to 2 m (5-6½ ft) higher than normal. But when a devastating hurricane strikes, the sea can be anything over 6 m (20 ft) higher than usual – easily as high as a house. Tidal surges often cause the greatest destruction.

Monitors

In the USA, hurricanes are watched by the National Hurricane Center. There are also official monitors in the West Indies (Bermuda), Cuba, Australia, India and Pakistan.

Eye,Eye!

The eye is a weird phenomenon bang in the centre of a hurricane. This is the calm area of the storm. The winds disappear and the clouds depart. The eye can hover over an area, creating an illusion of calm. Yet, at its edge, the winds are ferocious and after a while they return with devastating force. This could take minutes or even an hour.

Tornadoes

Hurricanes can often throw out tornadoes, which are also known as twisters in the USA. Cool, dry air on land meets the incoming warm, moist air of the hurricane and squeezes out a narrow band of air. The column is thrust down in a typical funnel shape, spinning at tremendous speed – anything from 116 kph (72 mph) to a terrific 420 kph (261 mph) – the most violent winds on earth!

This image shows what a tornado might look like as it heads towards you.

Tree Huggers

Many orchards in the southern states of the USA, such as Florida, Louisiana and the Carolinas, have survived hurricanes. Mature trees are vulnerable to damage, but young trees are so supple that they bend with the fierce wind. Surprisingly, most of the fruit stays on the trees – at worst only 5 per cent of the fruit would normally be lost.

Hurricanes
- The Biggies

Place: The Caribbean
Date: 1780
Top Windspeeds: unrecorded
Effect: Huge swathes of the Caribbean were
devastated when a series of very strong
hurricanes struck the region in rapid succession.
Three struck in the first three weeks of October.
The first struck Jamaica, creating huge waves
which flooded the port of Savanna la Mar.
A 'great Hurricane' then bombarded
Barbados a week later. Only ten houses were
left standing. The Hurricane then moved on to
six other islands, leaving a total death-toll of
20,000.

Place: Texas, USA
Date: 1900
Top Windspeeds:
209 kph (130 mph)
Effect: 6,000 were
killed and a storm
wave washed over
Galveston Island,
causing incredible
damage.

Place: Florida, USA
Date: 1928
Top Windspeeds:
258 kph (160 mph)
Effect: Between 6
September and 20
September,
1,836 were killed
in southern Florida
and 1,870 injured.
An entire lake, Lake
Ochebogee, overflowed
into the town of Okechobee, causing massive
floods and many deaths by drowning.

Place: Long Island and New England, USA
Date: 1938
Top Windspeeds: 295
kph (183 mph)
Effect: 600 were
killed and 1,754
injured when a
record-breaking
hurricane tore
through the Blue
Hills of
Massachusetts and the
surrounding area.

17

Place: United Kingdom
Date: 1962
Top Windspeeds:
198 kph (123 mph)
Effects: Only very
rarely is Britain hit
by hurricane-force
winds, but in
February 1962, a
hurricane-force wind hit
Lanarkshire in Scotland
and then sped south as far as
Sheffield. Over 7,000 houses were damaged. The
noise of the wind was so great, it was reckoned to
be the noisiest night since the blanket bombing of
Britain in the Second World War.

Place: United Kingdom
Date: 1987
Top windspeeds:
172 kph (107 mph)
Effects: On 27
March, twelve
people were killed
and dozens injured
when cars were
hurled off roads, tiles
blown off roofs and trains
brought to a halt as electric
cables were brought down. School classrooms
collapsed and thousands of trees were uprooted.
Part of the copper dome of the Old Bailey,
London's famous law court, was blown away.

Place: United Kingdom
Date: 1987 (again!)
Top Windspeeds: 177 kph (110 mph)
Effects: The hurricane winds of the 'great storm' of 15 October caused weather damage worth nearly £1 billion – the highest ever recorded in Britain's history. Many thousands of trees were blown down like matchsticks – even a tree at Kew Gardens which had survived every storm since 1761 was uprooted.

Place : North Carolina, USA
Date: 1996
Top Windspeeds:
185 kph (115 mph)
Effect: When Hurricane Fran moved north and hit Cape Fear, huge amounts of rain fell and tornadoes spun off the main hurricane. 28 people were killed and damage was put at a massive $1 billion.

WEIRD!

A hurricane's immense destructive force is no joke, but some strange and extraordinary things have nevertheless happened.

In a freak hurricane in 1938 in New England, USA, Mr and Mrs Livingston Gibson of Westhampton Beach climbed on to the roof of their house as the sea flooded the coast. Suddenly they, along with a small snake and three rats which had also climbed on to the roof, were swept out to sea. They ended up sailing across a bay, and landed on Westhampton golf course!

Clouds of insects, such as mosquitoes and tarantula spiders, have been blown in from farmlands and swamps in the Caribbean and ended up in the USA!

 So much fresh water poured into the salt-water bays when Hurricane Beulah hit the USA and Mexico in 1967, people could actually drink the salt water!

In Britain, during the 'The Great Tempest' of 23 November 1703, at St Peter's in Thanet, a cow was found alive after being blown into the top branches of a tree. The same night, from Sandwich to Canterbury in Kent, the riverbanks were littered with fish that had been blown out of the water!

In one hurricane, a row of birds sitting on the branches of a tree were still there after the hurricane – but they had lost all their feathers!